CSA

KU-362-932

WITHDRAWN

The Garden of Bad Dreams
and Other Stories

Also by Christopher Hope

FICTION
My Mother's Lovers
Separate Development
Kruger's Alp
The Hottentot Room
My Chocolate Redeemer
Serenity House
Darkest England
Me, the Moon and Elvis Presley
Heaven Forbid

SHORTER FICTION
Black Swan
Learning to Fly
The Love Songs of Nathan J. Swirsky

POETRY
Cape Drives
In the Country of the Black Pig
English Men

FOR CHILDREN
The King, the Cat and the Fiddle (with Yehudi Menuhin)
The Dragon Wore Pink

NON-FICTION
White Boy Running
Moscow! Moscow!
Signs of the Heart
Brothers Under the Skin

The Garden *of* Bad Dreams

and Other Stories

Christopher Hope

Atlantic Books
LONDON

First published in Great Britain in 2008 by
Atlantic Books, an imprint of Grove Atlantic Ltd.

Some of these stories have appeared before in slightly
different forms. 'In The Way' was published in the *New
Statesman*; 'Gus' in *New Contrast*; 'The Pink Shoes' in
Bad Sex. The following stories were commissioned by
the BBC and broadcast on Radio 3 and 4: 'The Garden
of Bad Dreams'; 'The White Witch'; 'Covered Bridge and
Autumn Splendour' ; 'Whose Zoo'; 'The Day Out'; 'How
It Was'; 'The Violin'.

1 3 5 7 9 8 6 4 2

A CIP catalogue record for this book is available from
the British Library.

ISBN: 978 1 84354 772 3

Printed in Great Britain by Cromwell Press Limited,
Trowbridge, Wiltshire.

Atlantic Books
An imprint of Grove Atlantic Ltd.
Ormond House
26–27 Boswell Street
London WC1N 3JZ

For Duncan, who travels

Danger and delight grow on one stalk.
Old English proverb

Contents

The Garden of Bad Dreams   1

The White Witch   14

Veterans   23

In the Way   36

The Pink Shoes   44

Whose Zoo   54

The Day Out   62

Wall Story   72

Covered Bridge and Autumn Splendour   77

How It Was   85

St Francis in the Veld   96

The Violin   110

Gus   120

The Garden of Bad Dreams

High in the hills of Buda, the Collector dreams of midgets. When I met him I thought he was mad. But he is simply obsessed. A meaty fellow in a rayon shirt who tends to weep easily. He talks of 'those who used to be, and who will be again'. Visionary talk.

There are men who will buttonhole you and pull from their wallets pictures of wives and kids, but for the midget fancier it is black-and-white photographs from another age: Budapest 1936. A group of people poses in the public gardens: men in hats with wide dipping brims; women in loose sleeves and floating hemlines. They belong to a troupe of twenty-eight artists in the Lilliputian Theatre, sometimes called the Hungarian Dwarf Theatre, in the days when disproportion of leg and head and physical form were not much bothered about – when small was small and you took your dwarfs with your midgets and didn't bother about which was which. What is so striking about those photographed in the

Budapest park is they are utterly easy with themselves. Tiny persons, perfect miniatures whose very easiness challenges us to see them differently and who seem to say: We are relaxed, we are normal, we are as we are. There is something daring, even dangerous, about the assurance with which they look into the camera. So pert, so heart-stoppingly unaware they are about to vanish. For ever.

The Collector's dream is to resurrect the old Lilliputian ensemble. The Dwarf Theatre will live again. Suitable small people are to be winkled out of the dark corners where they hide their beauty and if they pass his test of 'the true ones', he will keep them like silkworms in a shoebox.

'Here are pictures of my current six. You can see they still exist. Truly.'

Tonight he has a show on TV but he is still one midget adrift.

Everyone will tell you – from the dreamer in the hills to the salesman who 'travels' in small people, or the circus agent who finds them jobs – that there are crucial differences between gnomes, dwarfs and midgets. In the metaphysics of midgetry, gnomes are bucolic, elderly, fairy-tale creatures, sometimes associated with riches: as, say, the gnomes of Zurich. Dwarfs are less reliable, discomforting; they evoke sympathy but it is mixed with fear. They embody a condition. But midgets are perfect copies of 'us'. Parodies of the taller world.

'True midgets are so…' The Collector knots his fingers between his knees, looking for the word. 'Adorable!'

Hearing of a possible acquisition, we drive down from the hills and over the Danube on the wonderfully sturdy Chain Bridge that joins Buda to Pest. On the bridge a romantic has scrawled, 'Mary Loves Attila.'

It makes me wonder if Attila feels the same way.

In a café near the Parliament, a midget broker shows us samples of his present stock. He shuffles photos of potential candidates before slapping them down like cards on the coffee table, to the constant chant of 'No, no, no,' from the Collector. Of all the broker's stock only Marlis, a blonde in a low-cut black evening dress, who measures just 65 cm, passes muster.

'She's good,' says the broker. 'Take her.'

But the Collector is doubtful. 'If you look closely at the legs,' he says, 'you'll see more dwarf than midget.'

'She's on special,' says the salesman. 'A bargain. Times are tight and good ones scarce.'

But the Collector won't buy.

He is still short by one for the TV appearance tonight. We cross to Margaret Island, in the middle of the Danube. The guidebooks call it a peaceful pearl inside the frantic oyster of Budapest. There we consult a trainer of clowns who works for an out-of-town circus. Another expert, but not, certainly not, a romantic. The trainer has no midgets on his books now. He is baffled by the market for small people. When he wants them he can't find them, and when he finds them he can't place them. That is the paradox – there is no market for midgets, yet the best get snapped up.

'Now, in America, as I understand it, they used to throw dwarfs, but that's not the Hungarian way. Our circuses will still hire the occasional small man for shows in the provinces. And the movies offer a niche, now and then. But long term – well, there is no long term.'

The trainer promises to keep his eyes open but clearly he has little faith in the resurrection of the Lilliputian Theatre of Budapest. He does not believe that the man in the hills can pull it off. Like the salesman who travels in short people, he sees midgets as 'entities', rare to the point of extinction, which must fit some rare slot – or vanish.

'I hear there is perhaps a market now for such entities who are used for racing camels in rich desert kingdoms. You might try importing someone,' he says doubtfully.

We go to see a second midget middleman at the Hilton, on the river, and he shows us his line-up: two photos, two smiling small people. Bela – a jockey, who rides an ostrich, is no taller than a child of four, 'with quite perfect proportions'. And Tibor does 'impressions' – though of what or whom, the middleman does not say.

But neither Tibor nor Bela wants a stage career. They work free-lance. And they have other offers.

'See,' says the Collector, not in the least despondent, 'they do still exist.'

But the truth is that they do not do so with any comfort. To see them in their true pride you have to go back a long way. Open the heavy volumes of photos and postcards in the Hungarian National Library and they bounce from the pages, fresh and bright and assured. Marvellous entities from another universe, the Hungarian Dwarf Circus that delighted Moscow, Paris, Prague for decades. In one affecting image they are dressed as Prussian soldiers in white calico breeches and carry muskets, sabres, and wear brass helmets, posing in a little platoon before the Brandenburg Gate. Because this is Berlin, their attitude seems to say that a little martial flourish is in order. But the location lends a particular poignancy; the date is 1938. The little Prussian soldiers pose and preen. They are identified by name – Borodino, Wildman, Rolly and Zolika.

He is the one – Zolika.

Little Zoli they called him, or 'Zoli the Dwarf'. He would have reached no higher than my waistline. Of course, the troupe to which they belonged boasted all sorts of marvels: Jono who boxed horses; the Lion boy, just five years old, his face flourishing a golden beard, his hairy hands poking out of a blue silk tunic ornamented with flowers; Watson the Electric Phenomenon, who illuminated light bulbs with his fingers; and the Vivian brothers, *les maîtres de l'équilibre*, who mounted a ladder, balancing head to head on a bottle of champagne! But Zoli set the standard. He was the funniest, most famous small man in Europe.

He began life crying because the children mocked his tiny body and went on crying until he discovered what he called his 'profession'. He learnt to love the circus instead. Later, he fled Budapest for Amsterdam, helped by his friend Hans Kobert-Belling who made his name playing the matador in a midget *corrida*, using dogs dressed as bulls, fake horns, brass nose rings and all.

'Listen to me, Zoli,' said Hans. 'You shouldn't have to pay for your ticket from Vienna to Amsterdam. My dogs are booked into a separate carriage. A small man like you has enough space to bunk with them. No one would spot you. Trust me. You will travel to Cologne free and from there it is only a few steps to Amsterdam.'

We know Kobert-Belling offered him more sage advice…

'And get yourself some publicity photographs.'

Hidden with Kobert-Belling's dogs, Zoli was aiming for the heart of Europe. It very nearly ended in disaster. The train was stopped by heavy snow in Passau. Wearing his silk top hat, sitting on his suitcase, Zoli shivered through the night in the wooden waiting room. But he was on his way.

Zoli loved show, spectacle, glitter and greasepaint. He sat up all night in Moscow to see the sunrise; marvelled at Napoleon's cannonballs; he found Russian women adorable and they returned his passion. It is true that there were other artists who excited their fans, who drew applause and admiration – there was Miss Josla, who rode lions, and barefoot Harry, effortlessly pulling corks from champagne bottles, shooting a rifle and arranging flowers, all with his naked toes. They were all admired but Zoli was loved. He was the ultimate human toy – to fondle, dandle, to take home after the circus and keep in a box by your bed. Zoli outshone colleagues and compatriots and competitors: like Manfred, who gulped down live mice; or Gustav, who swallowed sabres, two at a time; or Rubber-Face Minnie and her singing dogs.

Little Zoli rose and rose in the estimation of those who laughed at him. He gambled, fooled and flirted his way across Europe. He joked with German princes and entranced the Tsar's court. In Venice he was mobbed by pigeons. In the ancient arena in Pompeii he played the toreador. He adored actresses and jewellery, cards and macaroni. He won and lost gold walking sticks and diamond rings. In Budapest he was so smitten by an opera singer that he and his small friends removed the horses from her carriage and pulled it themselves.

He wrote down his own story in a book called *Big Life, Little Man*. And it is all that remains of Zoli, but for the pictures in the Budapest National Library.

In this book you will find the major events of my strange and adventurous life. I tried to put down everything that might be interesting in the big life of a little man.

Yes, Ladies and Gentlemen, here is little Zoli, not with a painted face this time, not in the costume of a clown, hiding his real self and forcing himself to smile, but with a naked soul, the way he lives, the way he is happy, as he struggles all his life, just like you, Ladies and Gentlemen.

Big Life, Little Man is breathless, urgent and blazingly sentimental – the showbiz patter of a teeny ringmaster. And yet it is suffused with pain – best summed up by a kind of religious awakening, a vision one dark night in Budapest.

The Collector in the hills read me Zoli's account of his vision.

'Ladies and Gentlemen: here is what happened. One night I left the theatre late; the foyer was dark already when I stepped out to the street. I slowly started to walk towards the subway station, when from the shadows a tall, slim, badly dressed man stepped in front of me. I looked up at his hollow cheeks, which were darkened by the tucked-up collar of his coat. I was surprised for a second; maybe I was also scared that this man wanted to attack me. But the fear lasted only for a second, because the man started to talk to me in a timid voice:

"Excuse me, sir," he said. "Excuse me for disturbing you… I would like to ask a big favour from you… My son, Gabi… is very ill – he has pneumonia…" The fellow swallowed and I reckoned that he was hiding his tears, which were falling inside him. "The doctor told us tonight that he would not live until

7

morning… I am a poor man and I do not have a job at the moment and neither have I any money and… and I asked Gabi, how could I make him happy… and Gabi said, 'Father, please, call little Zoli from the circus, and I will be very happy then.' This is why I was waiting for you, this is why I came to the circus… Please, do not be angry with me, I know that you are paid to perform… But I cannot pay you, Mr Zoli… I do not have anything, but Gabi will die by tomorrow morning. I ask you, that this time, please dispense with the payment and come with me."

'Even in the darkness I clearly saw the spasm take him, like in a cramp, he was sobbing. And I felt something take hold of me, too, like an invisible hand choking me, something I've never felt before.

'A cloud covered the moon and there was a strong wind. It was a cold, unfriendly night. Somewhere there was a child in agony. I took the man's hand and all I could say was: "Let's go!"

'I never could remember the way we went on that night – I only remember some poor houses, dark and narrow streets, we went through a courtyard, then there was a door and after a few minutes I stood in the only room of this apartment. An old cupboard, three chairs and a bed. In the bed, covered with a striped quilt, I saw a boy of about nine or ten. There was an oil lamp in the room. I could see that on his cheeks there were these fever-roses, his eyes were glittering, his hair was wet, and covered his face. I remembered those smiling children at the circus earlier that evening, eating candies, pretzels or hot dogs. I saw now that there were other children – sad, ill "shadow-children". Suddenly I knew why I was here. To sweeten Gabi's last hours, to make him forget about the suffering, to make him laugh, to bring him – if only for a few minutes – the big present we are all looking for – happiness.

'It was the most difficult performance in my life. I went to his bed. I started to talk to him, I took his hot hand, and then I started to make fun, to joke around. That night God was with me… Because I did it. I got a smile on those pale lips, I was jumping and joking in front of his bed, and he laughed. I was inspired. Maybe I never played better. I remembered the best things from my repertoire, what made adults and children laugh from their hearts. Later on I sat beside him, holding his hands. I told him about dwarfs, trolls, kings and beautiful fairy queens. And all the while the father, this sad man, was standing by the door, watching his son. After a long time he suddenly said to me, "He's asleep now."

'Ladies and Gentlemen, when sometimes I wonder why I live on earth, whether there is any point to my strange difficult life, then I remember Gabi. I wonder whether he remembers that strange night when I played only for him. I like to think I had a hand in his recovery. He did not die that night, maybe because with my jokes I could grab him from the gate of death and draw him back to life. Ladies and Gentlemen, if little Zoli did not do anything important in his life, if in the big book of heaven they refuse to write down that for decades he gave moments of happiness to the anxious people in Budapest, and other cities all over the world, then one line is sure to make it into the book: "He saved Gabi."

'Ladies and Gentlemen, as years passed by, I realised that

God, who gave everyone a profession, gave me the duty to bring joy to you, to make you and your children laugh.'

The Collector in the big house in the hills of Buda stops reading and weeps; he is deeply affected by the story of Little Gabi. He loves small people, he wishes to conserve them, to make them live again.

One day, he tells me, a gang of very tall supermen marched into Budapest. They bent down and contemplated the Lilliputians. What was the purpose of these pygmies? Lilliputians in the world of the supermen were surplus to requirements. And very disturbing. They had an eerie effect on adults at the best of times and the tanks that rolled into Budapest were full of the tallest, most grown-up, least easily amused, strongest, most modern men the world had ever known. And so midgets were officially abolished.

Thrown on to the streets, Zoli scraped a living by hawking a basket filled with copies of *Big Life, Little Man* around the pubs and cafés of Budapest. For a while he survived, before he was netted like a butterfly and sent to a place run by the tall to do away with the small. It was a place with lots of children.

And what did Zoli do? He went on doing what he always did. He ignored the wretched advice of the tall, the hateful counsels of height and might. In the dark place he danced, he vamped, he fell over. He reprised his famous sketches: the Monkey and the English Bobby; the Sultan and the little Dutch Girl. He mimicked Miss Josla who rode lions; or Harry who had no arms but was clever with his feet – always formally dressed in black tie and tails, pulling corks from champagne bottles or shooting a rifle with his bare toes; or Joe, who hammered nails through his tongue.

In the dying light, Zoli the dwarf kept playing for the doomed shadow-children. What else was there to do until he perished with them?

The Collector drove me to an unsurprising suburb on a hillside above the city – a quiet place, where washing flapped in the gardens, and the houses were small. Its unrelieved domesticity was the point. How do sanguine ogres like to be kept in confinement in an atmosphere of soap suds and tricycles and prams and footballs, and utter ordinariness?

'It should have gone better for everyone,' said the Collector, 'when the Germans left. But then – would you believe it? – the Liberators arrived. And they were almost as tall and every bit as much trouble as the invaders they replaced. Worse, they had very high ideals. Not to mention a very ambitious policy of social uplift- ment. Mind you, there were very few midgets left to uplift. So many had gone the way of Zoli. A few remained but their rarity did not help them, they did not measure up. Small people, sports of nature and other anomalies fell short of the demands of the glorious revolution. Small was not only not beautiful, small was counter-revolutionary. And so midgets were officially abolished all over again. In 1946, the Lilliputian Theatre of Budapest closed for ever.

The Collector from Buda smiles slowly. 'Getting rid of midgets didn't mean we got rid of midgetry. Of course not. It just meant that little countries now took over from little people. Hungary and Czechoslovakia and Romania were all offered very small parts in the giant revolution, with Mother Russia directing. When our Director was pleased she gave us tall statues that we planted all

11

over the place – when we didn't do what she wanted, she sent in the tanks. Now that is over. Again. But everyone here knows that if you forget the giants, they will go on troubling your sleep, so it is better to keep them somewhere. Somewhere safe.'

We got out of the car and stood in front of very big gates and a tall wall. The giants of uplift and ambition live out their twilight in a muddy park above the city of Budapest. A monumental front gate, always kept locked, ensures that the visitor must seek out another entrance because where Soviet friendship was concerned, nothing was ever straightforward. This is a museum of mimicry. A loudspeaker at the entrance broadcasts socialist hymns sung by factory workers and vintage political speeches of party leaders.

These heroic hulks, marbles and bronze soldiers, peasants, workers, martyrs, many Lenins and even more Marxes stare solemnly into neighbouring gardens. Gods put out to grass, watching the washing, reminded always of their embarrassing proximity to ordinary lives. And as we pass amongst them we are led in a figure of eight back to the entrance by which we could not come in.

No more than about ten minutes after we have found our way in, the park keeper comes and tells us it is time to leave.

'But we've just got here,' says the Collector. 'Is it closing time?'

'It is always closing time,' says the park keeper. 'In the garden of bad dreams.'

In the TV studio that evening, the man who loves midgets is wearing a white frock with puffy sleeves and his stubble shows blue through the studio make-up; his wig is black, his shoes are shiny. He is rather tearful, and he is followed by a file of midgets wearing red pointed caps and pointed red noses. They start singing – what else? 'Hey-ho… Hey-ho, it's off to work we go…'

To begin with the audience is shocked, then amused but incredulous. It is hardly surprising they are astonished because they are expected to take this travesty seriously and to respond with warmth and love to the revival of the Lilliputian Theatre. But the audience does not remember the Lilliputians who delighted so many. They know only what they are seeing and they have seen the movie. They know the words of the song. It has come to this, a man in a frock leading a troupe of chanting manikins. I can hear the unspoken question forming in the spatters of sharp laughter. Sometimes – just possibly – life mimics art. OK. But when it apes Hollywood… forget it!

Zoli wrote in *Big Life, Little Man, 'This laughter hurt me sometimes, especially when I was young, and you might believe me when I say that I often cried in my pillow at that time, if there was a pillow under my head at all…'*

The laughter of the audience is shrill and hot, like the manic whistle of a boiling kettle.

Yet I want him to win, this large, weepy man in the frock and the five-o'clock stubble, I like his nerve. I hope Zoli might have approved. I can't help feeling, though, that the dreamer missed a trick when he turned down Marlis and failed to bring up the numbers to the magic seven. She may not have been perfect, but she was on special. Round and round they go under the implacable studio lights – Snow White shadowed by just six dwarfs.

The White Witch

I remember her tiny feet, her flair and her bravery. She lived in the mountains where nothing looked the same when the mist came down, and yet she summed up the possibility of not just becoming someone else but of inhabiting an identity so successfully that she convinced the only person that mattered – herself.

The construction of the tribal stockade, plank by plank, is available to settled peoples only. They know what they are because they know where they are. For others, and there are more and more 'others', leaving the safety of the defensive huddle means there is no going back. Becoming someone else, somewhere else, is what they do.

'You try a lot of places until you pass off one as your own,' was how Jimmy Li Fu put it.

He said it as if I didn't have any problem just being who I was and not having to pass myself off as anyone in particular. Didn't have to work at it. People like me were privileged.

I didn't quite see it that way. My family left London for Kuala Lumpur in the 1930s. They went into rubber and tea, just as other settlers in other places went into gold or jute or timber, and sent the loot 'home'. They lived in the land they grew to love and believed it was theirs. It wasn't and they, too, were sent 'home'. That was rough: if there is something stranger than a country you do not know, it is the utter foreignness of old familiar streets when the names change.

I suppose I went back to Malaysia pretty often in order to guess at what would have become of me had they stayed. I also went back to see my friends who were, for the most part, citizens but not 'sons of the soil' in the 'new' Malaysia. I went, in particular, to visit Jimmy Li Fu, up in the Cameron Highlands.

He was by origin Straits Chinese, but he was always telling me he was 'a real' Malaysian, though I'd never suggested otherwise. He grew up in the Chinese gangs of KL, and once showed me his tattoo, a red dragon on a green field.

'If you had the wrong tattoo, you were gone. If you ended up in someone's gang, then they made the rules. You learnt to play the game or you were dead.'

That was what gave him his belief that he was a fully genuine, entirely legitimate, 'one hundred thousand per cent' Malaysian – when it clearly wasn't so. Yet he swore to it, and so did everyone he knew, and I could see what they were driving at. It was the game you learnt to play.

'Do you think emigrants are good actors?'

'Wrong question,' said Jimmy. 'Are we guests or ghosts?'

I thought of that as I drove into the Highlands, leaving behind the heat of the plain and heading for the mountains. The air cooled quickly as I climbed. I skirted a boulder the size of a small house that had fallen on to the road. It rained a lot in the hills and as the jungle was stripped away, more and more landslides came to call. Wisps of mist laced the windscreen. The mist was a familiar in the Cameron Highlands, like the cloud and the rain. They called it the White Witch.

I was aiming for Brinchang, and the Marlborough Arms. It's a little half-timbered place, just past the Victoria and Albert Butterfly Farm, and it belongs to Jimmy Li Fu. You'll see him from time to time in the tea-garden of the V&A. Sometimes one of his girls is with him – young, slim, silent. Chances are Jimmy is on his mobile, talking to his bookie in Singapore.

Orang asli people sat by the road, hawking blowpipes and potted jungle plants. They were here long before the Malays, the Chinese, the Tamils and the British. They were trackers and collectors of bark. They made incense from eaglewood, and scented sandalwood and aloe liquor. They sold oil from the cassava tree; camphor for headaches and stomach pains; they traded honey and beeswax smelling of toffee and ash. Now they came and went in the mist, like the wraiths they were.

Below Tanah Rata, beside a stretch of muddy water, a mock-Tudor mansion shouldered its way out of the mist. A surreal reminder of the nostalgic dreams of those who once colonized these high-altitude Home Counties. The rubber planters came for the cool consolation of the Camerons. Then followed soldiers, clerics and civil servants – the roses and radishes brigade, some called them. And if it wasn't ever quite home, if it was an England run rampant, then at least there were golf, gin, Jaguar motor cars and whole mountainsides of tea.

How well those monuments hung on. The mist was toying with the Inglenook Souvenir Stall, switching it on and off. In Tanah Rata high street, a pink neon sign read ABIGAIL'S DEVONSHIRE CREAM TEAS. Abigail had been the aged cousin of an even older aunt, the last of my relatives in Malaysia. The owners now were colleagues of Jimmy Li Fu, and Abigail's now mixed toby jugs and joss sticks, Chinese lanterns and cupcakes, oriental home comforts with the exotic sweetmeats of inscrutable Albion.

It was late afternoon by the time I got to Brinchang and sat in the snug of the Marlborough Arms, drinking Singapore slings with Jimmy Li Fu. The Marlborough had it all. Horse brasses on the wall, the Queen Mum over the fireplace – and yet it wasn't cosy, or quaint or genteel. On the contrary, it had an almost bawdyhouse feeling. It is jarring when the sedate morphs into the overripe. Sitting in the snug of the Marlborough, ringed by foxhunting prints, I could have been in a massage parlour.

Jimmy Li kept the cooking in the old exotic tradition. There was Lancashire hotpot on the menu, and plum duff to follow. These were his specialities: boarding-school puddings. Jam roly-poly, spotted dick, apple crumble.

I asked Jimmy Li, 'Why does the sight of Abigail's Cream Teas, and the fish-and-chip shops in Tanah Rata town, seem so weird? Why does what is not in the least romantic look so wild, so… over-heated when you see it here?'

'Wrong question,' said Jimmy Li. 'You mean – what happens to people like us?'

17

'People like us?'

'Sure. You and me. Nowhere people. You know why the Chinese love Malaysia? Because we're free to make money. But that's all. We don't count. They don't care what we do because they don't care who we are. As you British showed when you ran the country. You only count if you push people about. Now you're gone. Who cares? But the bits you left behind still smell strong – golf, tea, grey-hounds. The frilly bits.'

I knew the frilly bits. Anglican churches and Tudor fronts and Austins winding up to the tea estates. But greyhounds seemed to be stretching it. If you race greyhounds you need a track. I'd never heard of a greyhound track, up there in the jungle.

'Would I lie to you?' said Jimmy Li.

'Certainly.'

'All right – would I lie to you about something important? It is simply that Captain Moresby raced dogs long ago. His wife's still alive, over at Honeysuckle Cottage. Go see for yourself. If you want to know what happens to people like us, ask her. It's an easy walk.' He put his phone to his ear. 'Better take a torch, the Witch is out.'

Walking in the forest was menacingly easy. Many old trails threaded through the trees. They had been made, Jimmy had once told me, by the Communists during the Emergency. I used one still marked CLOSED, and the mist lapped at my knees, rising and falling in silky waves. While it stayed low, it was OK. But I needed the torch. The Witch could swaddle and swallow you whole. Novice walkers abruptly slipped away and, in a last hope of finding them, the police would call out the *Orang asli* trackers.

Honeysuckle Cottage was on a slope above Tanah Rata. It was

made of corrugated iron, painted dark green, with a white wooden gable and long verandahs. There were great festoons of honeysuckle over the windows and doors. The rose garden was particularly beautiful, a series of terraces flowing down to a smooth lawn. Where the lawn ended, the jungle began.

She was in the back yard, bottling strawberry jam. She wore baggy grey flannels, a brown dust coat of the sort you once saw on janitors, and an old Panama hat. Her hands on the jars were quick and dainty.

'I'm so pleased to see someone from the old country.'

Poking out from under her gray flannels were little red slippers, about five inches long. I know those tiny shoes. There is a Chinese cobbler down Jonkers Street in Malacca who still makes shoes for elderly Chinese women who had their feet bound as girls. Her feet stuck out beneath her grey flannels like little trotters.

She held out her hand. 'Betty Moresby.'

'Would I lie to you?' Jimmy Li had asked.

He hadn't needed to. I was in the Highlands where lies are like the mist.

We drank tea in front of the fire. On the mantelpiece was a photograph of a large blond man with a big moustache, and another of Hampstead Ponds. She looked at me looking at them.

'My husband – Captain Moresby. Archie was a London man.'

She spoke with that drawl that was once fashionable in upper middle-class English circles. 'A London maahn…'

A painting of a women of about thirty, very blonde and soft and somehow sad, hung over the fireplace.

'That's Alice. Archie's first wife. She was from Devon. Devonshire is a particularly beautiful part of the world, is it not?'

Devon was indeed beautiful in parts. She wasn't asking a question, she was claiming Devon as her heritage.

I asked her when she was last in England.

'We had planned a trip. Archie wanted me to see Hampstead. He wanted to walk on the Heath, we were going to have a drink at Jack Straw's Castle. Afterwards, there didn't seem much point.'

I asked about Captain Moresby's greyhounds. Was there a track?

'Certainly there was a track! In Tapah. Where the ornamental gardens are. They raced on Friday nights. The soldiers from the barracks came, as did lots of locals.'

The ornamental gardens. A green space where sedate families paraded on Sundays. It was odd to think of the dog track, lost under the palms and the orchids and the lilies.

'People used to putter up from KL for the racing. But the fighting in the Emergency put a stop to all that. Archie had trouble getting breeding stock from Home.'

Her small hands were lovely on the teapot. 'Dalton,' she said.

Betty Moresby had taken on English colouration; she mixed it from her husband's culture, his clothes, his accent. People who have fallen in love with other places sometimes speak the new language with exaggerated care. If it's German, they boom away in a Wagnerian fashion. If they go Chinese, they speak Mandarin with mincing correctness. They select the one feature that sums up the character they wish to impersonate and they over-emphasize. They perform and, like many converts, they overact.

But this was a performance of steely calm. Betty Moresby was Chinese, we were high in the mountain jungles of Malaysia, and I could not take my eyes off her tiny bound feet in her red shoes. Yet everything was as it should be, she'd made it so, and there was something implacable in her determination to keep it so. She *was* Captain Moresby's widow, in old grey flannels, spooning cream on to my scones to eat with her home-made jam. Poking the fire with what I felt sure must have been an English poker.

'Archie always used to say we'd retire to Hampstead. I believe Hampstead is very desirable?'

I said it was. Very.

'I thought so.' She seemed pleased. 'Archie's buried in All Souls. Would you like to see his memorial?'

We walked down to the little Church of All Souls, on the edge of the jungle. It is really an old Nissen hut. The lychgate was a memorial to Miss Gwinny Griffith-Jones. I wondered if she too had been Chinese.

Betty Moresby's plaque to her husband was near the altar. 'At the going down of the sun, and in the morning…'

The date was 1960. Captain Moresby had been dead nearly forty years.

That evening I sat in the snug at the Marlborough Arms and drank gin slings, and Jimmy Li told me about her. She'd been called Tang Yun back then, and she was Straits Chinese. Archie Moresby had taken up with her weeks after his wife died. Tang Yun had been only seventeen and there'd been a scandal at the time.

'So he hid her. He kept her under wraps. In all the time they were married, you never saw them together in public. It was only when he died that she began to come out.'

'To come out?'

'Yes. Just that. Getting to be who he said she was. There was no holding her.'

21

I thought again of those tiny red slippers.

On my last night in the Cameron Highlands, I dined with Betty Moresby at the Marlborough Arms. She wore a pale blue frock and her tiny feet were beautiful in pale blue slippers. Beef Wellington on the menu. Mrs Moresby said Wellington was a man whose legend she revered. She sent her compliments to the chef.

Jimmy Li Fu came out of the kitchen in his chef's hat and kissed her hand.

'Good evening, Mrs M.,' he said.

'Good evening, James,' said Betty Moresby.

We finished with Jimmy's famous jam roly-poly, and she talked to me about the Royal Family.

'It's so nice to meet someone of like mind,' said Betty Moresby.

I left for KL early the next morning. The tea plantations glowed green in the creamy mist. Nothing is what it seems when the Witch is out. Not even something like tea. Tea seems safe and familiar but tea is also a drug. Tea is a bush that wants to be a tree. So you must cut it back all the time.

'No one cares what we do because no one cares who we are,' said Jimmy Li Fu.

In Tanah Rata, Abigail's flashed its pink neon like a stripper. On the pavement an *Orang asli* hunter hawked jungle honey packed in old Coke bottles, slung from a rope like smoked kippers. A line of blowpipes dangled in the window of the Olde England Tea & Coffee Shoppe, and the early mist waved like lace curtains. I might have been leaving some English coastal resort – Bognor or Scarborough. Except for the size of the moths. And the frilly bits.

Veterans

When Swirsky came back to Badminton it was spring. The light looked smoky blue and seemed to float in the red earth gardens, and over the sandy roads, all named for English kings and queens. On our estate the houses were small, the gardens were hard to dig and everything was new. Some of our fathers had been working in their gardens, wearing bits of their old army uniforms, sieving fractious bits of shale from the red earth, bossing their black gardeners, or killing khaki worm. Sometimes, in the late afternoons, they went down to the ex-servicemen's club and talked about Montgomery and Rommel, and how bally awful our government was, and how it would never last past 1955. Then they went home and bossed the gardeners some more.

I was playing cricket on the lawn with Tony. He was batting; I was bowling. The lawn was lumpy kikuyu grass, and the ball jumped a lot. Sally wasn't playing because she bowled underhand – long flat rolling balls called 'coolie-creepers'.

Sally said to me, 'Why won't you let me bowl, Martin?'

'Because you do coolie-creepers.'

'So?'

'It's not allowed, that's all.'

'You're just scared!'

Tony said, 'There's Mr Swirsky!'

I didn't believe him until he pointed and then we looked and there he was, driving down Henry Avenue, in a blue A-40, with the driver's window rolled down, and his arm out of the window and the hair black and thick on his wrist. He didn't stop or wave or anything but we knew it was Mr Swirsky. His moustache was very black, like always.

'Maybe he's been to Wimbledon?' said Tony.

We knew what he meant. Ruthie Swirsky came from Wimbledon to Africa to marry Mr Swirsky, but then she went off with a singer on a motorbike. We sometimes thought she might have gone back to Wimbledon. But Ruthie Swirsky was not with him. If he had been away to look for her then he hadn't found her.

We stopped playing and I went home. My father was in the garden, planting out some strelitzias. He pulled off his army cap, he scratched his head, and he leaned on his garden fork.

'Your strelitzia loves cool, deep holes and some stones around the roots. I don't suppose you're here to help, are you?'

I waited for him to say something about Mr Swirsky but he didn't.

I went inside, and my mother said, 'I'm very worried about the sanitary lanes. They're absolutely teeming by night! The servants sit there, they light fires, and they play drums. I lie in bed and listen and worry myself sick.'

I said, 'We can't see them, they're behind the walls.'

My mother said, 'But I can hear them. Some of them even sing! Those lanes were not built for servants to have fun in – were they? Bally cheek! If I wanted an orchestra in my back yard, I'd jolly well ask for one.'

I said, 'I saw Mr Swirsky. Driving down Henry Avenue.'

My mother's eyes went as round as shillings. 'Nathan Swirsky? Back in Badminton! I suppose he went off into the big wide world and the big wide world wasn't wide enough for him.'

The next morning Tony and Sally and me went up to the shops and there was Papas at the Greek Tea Room, standing out on the pavement, talking to Mr Benjamin the Rug Doctor.

When Papas saw us he said, 'Well, kids, guess what the wind blew in?'

On the pavement were the wooden boards that had covered up the window of Swirsky's chemist shop ever since he had gone away. Swirsky was in the window, wearing his white coat, the thick creamy one that made my lips water, and on the floor he was building a highway, using bottles of California Syrup of Figs. The road was wide, and it went from one wall to the other in a big wavy snake, and Swirsky had written inside the shop window, in shaving cream:

'Take Syrup of Figs! The Road to Regularity!'

When Swirsky finished the road, he turned around and gave us a big bow.

'Let's go inside,' said Sally.

He was behind the counter, and I asked him, 'Did you go to Rhodesia, Mr Swirsky? Did you stay at the Leopard Rock Motel? We phoned you at the Leopard Rock Motel. But you weren't there.'

'Been and gone, probably,' said Swirsky. 'The Leopard Rock is as good as ever. No frost, no mosquitoes, no bilharzia. Let me tell you, frankly, you can't beat Rhodesia! Fastest-growing country of the British Empire. Opportunities for the willing worker. Thousands arriving monthly! So here's a tip, Martin, if ever you're up Rhodesia way, book early and stay at the Leopard Rock Motel.'

Sally asked him, 'Why can't I bowl coolie-creepers, Mr Swirsky?'

'Because they have a bad name. They keep low and swerve about. Very tricky ball to play, your coolie-creeper.'

Sally went and stood close to him and he rubbed the top of her head. I'd forgotten how soft and pink his hands were.

'You look like a traveller to me, my girl. Remember – if ever you're at the Victoria Falls and they can't fit you in at the Leopard Rock, then you can't beat Livingstone. A fine little *ville*, just seven miles from Vic Falls. Air connections to every part of the world. Try the Stanley Hotel, lovely place. Mention my name.'

Sally shook her head. 'They wouldn't take me – I'm only seven.'

'They'd take you, sweetheart, all you need to do is smile. And tell 'em Nathan Swirsky sent you.'

Tony said, 'Were you in Rhodesia for all the time, Mr Swirsky?'

'Some of the time, boykie. Northern and Southern Rhodesia. Yes. And points north. In fact, I went just about everywhere: Taj Mahal… Tierra del Fuego. But I've come down to earth with a bump.'

It was hard to think he'd bump. He was darker and rounder and pinker than ever and his moustache was very fine. When Swirsky came down to earth, he would bounce.

He took us out to his car, and it was full of boxes.

'Give us a hand, men. My car's groaning with stock.'

We helped him move boxes of Carter's Little Liver Pills and Dr

Mackenzie's Veinoids and Oupa Headache Powders into his shop. When we'd finished he pulled a lot of barley-sugar walking sticks out of a jar.

'Get your lips around those!'

Papas came over from the Greek Tea Room, and Swirsky said, 'You should travel, Nick. It clears the head.'

'Travel is what I did,' said Papas. 'All the way from Alexandria I came. All the way from Greece I travelled.'

'That was long ago.'

'Not long ago enough for me,' said Papas.

'If ever you're in London,' said Swirsky to Tony, 'see the sights, by all means. The Thames… the Tower. But avoid Wimbledon, if you can. Deadly.'

We remembered Ruthie Swirsky. She came all the way from Wimbledon to marry Mr Swirsky. She liked her Africa raw. She'd liked Cape Town; she'd thought Cape Town was another Nice. Only it wasn't.

We remembered. But we didn't say.

When I got home, my mother said, 'What's the bet Nathan Swirsky went into the world, and bit off more than he could chew? Now he just waltzes back and thinks he can take up where he left off. Well, Badminton isn't what it was.'

I tried to think what it was that made Badminton not what it was. But everywhere I looked it was what it was, except that when Swirsky had gone away, they had boarded up his pharmacy and we had missed him. But everything else was the same. Our fathers tried to forget they had been soldiers but they couldn't. Everyone talked about 'before the War' and 'after the War'. The burglars still lived in the blue gums by the little river. The big watchdogs called Nero and

Caesar and Tiger still bit the dustbin men and the coal men and the neighbours and each other. Our fathers still kept their service revolvers hidden in their sock drawers, in case the burglars came along at night and hooked clothes off the chairs with fishing lines: Their 'demob' suits that they had been given when they had left the army still hung in their cupboards. The water truck still sprayed the sandy streets on Wednesdays, and Mr Moosah, the sammy, came with his vegetable truck on Fridays; and Errol the topsoil man still rolled down Henry Avenue in his lorry on Mondays, with Reggie, his albino boy, wearing his khaki hat with the green brim and his dark glasses and sitting on the mountains of topsoil,

The only thing that changed was the servants. They rolled in and out like waves on the beach.

We had a new one. Her name was Maggie and she moved around the table, lifting the lids of the pots of pumpkin and the potatoes, and my father kept saying, 'That's all right, Maggie, you just put the pots on the table, I take off the lids, OK, my girl? D'you savvy?'

For the rest nothing much changed, the days got clear and blue as spring went on, and my father worried about overwatering his larkspurs.

'Overwatering can be fatal,' he said. He had just taken a fresh load of topsoil from Errol, and the heap was piled dark and rich on the lawn. He stood there in his long army shorts and his short grey socks, swinging the hosepipe and looking at the soil with a look that said if that soil wasn't sieved fine as flour, Errol could take the lot back.

Errol said, 'It's fine as flour, boss.' Then he said, 'You got some work for my cousin, boss? Vijay's looking for a job. He has to leave the Free State. It's a problem.'

'What's he done?'

Errol said, 'It's not what he's done, it's what he is. He's Indian.'

'I can see that. Why's it a problem?'

Errol told him why, and my father said, 'Streuth! Are you sure about this, Errol?'

And Errol said, 'Yes boss.'

Gus Trupshaw came over and my father said, 'Did you know Indians aren't allowed in the Free State?'

'What – not a single one?' said Gus Trupshaw.

'Not a bloody one. By law. It's some tradition they have. It goes back to the Boers. When they had the Free State as a republic. The Boers said they weren't having so much as an Indian toe on their land. So the entire bally province is Indian free.'

'You'd expect a few to slip through, Asians are slippery chaps.'

'Only Errol's cousin ever slipped through.'

'True's God?'

'Would I make this up, Gus?'

'I'm not doubting you, Gordon, but just him? On his lonesome?'

'I'm telling you. The only damn Indian in all the Free State.'

'But, Gordon, man, you would have thought he'd like stand out. Being the only one.'

'*Ja*, you would have thought so. But he was in some *dorp*, in the middle of nowhere. And it's full of farmers and they don't notice much. He was just like – part of the scenery. You know how it is…'

'I know how it is,' said Gus Trupshaw. 'It's like when you get a new domestic, and you put her in the girl's room in the back yard. But she doesn't stay there, not at first. She keeps jumping into your sight. It's about a month before you stop noticing her. And then it's like she isn't there. *Ja*, I understand that. And what do the guys in some Free State *dorp* know, anyway? Some bloke they don't look at twice. Maybe he's got a bit of gold in his teeth, or he's a bit dark. Or he's always eating curry. But they don't know, do they? They don't see him. They don't say – hey, there's a bloody Indian!'

'Apparently a new Dutch Reformed minister came to town. He spotted him. And it was overs-cadovers for Vijay.'

Gus Trupshaw laughed. 'Must have given them a bloody fright, hey? Someone new comes along and says, "Hey, did you people know you got a bloody coolie living next door?"'

'So Errol's cousin had to go. He's against the law. Bloody odd, isn't it?'

'Maybe they got a point, Gordon. Maybe they got scared about being overrun.'

'One Indian in the whole damn Free State! How's he going to overrun anyone?'

'Not now, maybe. But later. Just you wait. Take your eye off these guys for a minute and there's twenty more where you last looked. They breed like rabbits. It's like India.'

'Errol wanted to know if I had some work for him.'

Gus Trupshaw drew in his breath, big and strong. He hit himself on his forehead with his big brown hand. 'Sheez, Gordon, man! You can't keep him. Not in the same yard. What about your new domestic?'

'What about her?'

'She's a native, isn't she? Natives and Indians don't mix. It's a fact! Turn your back and in two ticks they'll be stabbing and burning each other. True's bob! Just like they did in Natal. You'll be having race riots in your own back yard.'

When she heard of this plan, my mother said, 'I'm not having it.

30

It's bad enough seeing servants thronging the sanitary lanes all night long. I do not want to wake up and find an Indian in my garden, thank you very much.'

My father had a beer with Swirsky, down at the ex-servicemen's club. They drank straight from the bottles and flipped their beer-bottle tops into the paraffin drum in the corner. My father said, 'Well, Natie, long time no see. Where you been all this time, man?'

'Here and there,' said Swirsky. 'I was in Pretoria quite a bit. It's a pretty little town, full of history and statuary.'

'History and statuary.' My father whistled the way he did when he was impressed but didn't believe something and didn't want to say so.

They pulled at their beers and Swirsky advised my father to use Union Castle boats when next he went to London.

My father told him about Errol's cousin. 'I feel sorry for the poor bastard. The only living Indian in the Free State – and now he's slung out on his ear. But I can't keep him. The missus would go dilly. Maybe you could use a servant? Now that you're back in civilization.'

'I'll ponder on that, Gordon,' said Mr Swirsky.

Later my father told my mother what Swirsky said about Pretoria and she was livid. 'History and statuary! What a damn nerve that man has! Marches in here cool as you please, and starts telling us where to get off! Now he wants a servant? Why? He's never kept one before. He always gave me the impression he was too grand to have a servant. Too much trouble for Mr Swirsky. Too infra dig to have to train them. No one could do things the way Nathan J. Swirsky wanted them. Now he's taking an Indian domestic. Well, really, it's too much!'

When we went round to Swirsky's pharmacy he was busy

decorating his window. He had someone helping him tie together bottles of Zulu Blood Purifier and packets of Meloids, to make a big bridge that looped across the full length of the pharmacy window. Swirsky's helper wore a creased tunic jacket with medals on his chest. He wore an army cap and when Swirsky shouted 'Attention!' he stood up very straight in the shop window and saluted.

'This is Mr Vijay Govender,' said Swirsky, 'He is my batman. And this is the Golden Gate Bridge we're building. The original is in San Francisco. One of the wonders of the modern world. Right, Mr Govender?'

'Yessir!' said Mr Govender. And he saluted again.

'Carry on, Mr Govender.'

Mr Govender went back to building the Golden Gate Bridge and Swirsky took us into his house and poured tall glasses of Lemos. We sat on his verandah and looked at the loquat tree and sipped our drinks through long thin naked straws.

'This is the life!' said Swirsky. 'Next time. I'll have my batman make the drinks.'

'What's a batman?' Tony said.

'A batman is someone who looks after an officer. He presses his clothes, shaves him, polishes his boots and cooks his meals.'

'Like a servant?'

'A bit. Except a batman is a soldier. A military man. Mr Govender was a military man. He is not a servant. Mr Govender lived all his life in the little town of Uitkyk, in the Free State, without anyone casting aspersions. Then he went to fight in the War. He came back from the War, and aspersions were cast. I plan to make it up to Mr Govender, he deserves better from his country.'

It caused a scandal in Badminton because Vijay Govender lived in Mr Swirsky's house and everyone said a servant's place was in the back yard.

Swirsky said, 'Let me say again: he's not a servant, he's a veteran, just like every other man on this estate, and he is billeted in my headquarters.'

My mother said, 'Next thing you know the servants will be wanting tea in bed!'

It caused another scandal when Mr Swirsky and Vijay Govender went walking in Henry Street wearing their caps, and saluted each other. As chairman of the ex-servicemen's league, Gus Trupshaw was asked to have a few words with Swirsky.

'It sets a dicey example, white people saluting black people.'

'Vijay Govender is of inferior rank. He salutes first,' said Swirsky. 'I merely return his salute.'

'We know that and you know that. But do the servants know that?' Gus Trupshaw said. 'They're simple chaps. They might get it into their thick heads that you are saluting first. Then what? Where will it end?'

Gus Trupshaw was right. It turned out that a lot of servants on the estate had also fought in the War and now they began wearing bits of their service gear, a pair of boots, a cap, a Sam Browne, just like our fathers did when they were working in their gardens, and cursing the heat and the shale and the flies. Then the servants also started saluting each other, just like Mr Swirsky and Mr Govender. And marching around sometimes, carrying bits of broomstick for guns. We used to go and watch them because they also sang *'Inkosi Sikelele' Africa'*, and 'God Save the King'…

The Badminton Ex-Servicemen's League held a crisis meeting in our kitchen and my mother made sausage rolls and Gus Trupshaw was there and he kept saying, 'Hell. The old s-h-one-t has hit the old f-a-n,' and my mother said, 'If you please, no language in this house.'

The league asked Errol the topsoil man to come and see them and Gus Trupshaw told him straight, 'Your cousin Vijay is making trouble, you must take him away.'

Errol said he couldn't do that. 'Please, boss, I only just got him here. Got nowhere to take him to.'

That's when the police drove their van into the estate and parked outside the Greek Tea Room, and watched the black servants marching with their broomsticks.

My father went round to Swirsky's pharmacy and said, 'For Christ sake's, Natie. Now the cops are here!'

Swirsky said, 'They don't scare me. This is plain intimidation. These chaps parading are ex-soldiers. They fought for their country same as we did. Why shouldn't they march?'

My mother said, 'That Nathan Swirsky's going to end up in the back of the Black Maria, if he isn't careful.'

It was Vijay Govender who remembered how he'd been the only Indian in the Free State, and the trouble there was when he got noticed, and everyone was noticing him now. He went to see Gus Trupshaw and next thing Mr Govender had left the estate.

Swirsky said, 'Dammit, I lost a fine batman and the forces of darkness have triumphed. I think it's terrible to lose an old soldier. We fought in the war together.'

'Some of these Indians are smart,' Gus Trupshaw told my father. 'I found him a job on the other side of town. In Fordsburg.'

'Good one, Gus, Fordsburg's knee deep in Indians.'

'Exactly, Gordon. They'll never notice another one. And now maybe life can get back to normal.'

But the black ex-servicemen went on marching and life did not get back to normal. After more meetings it was agreed that the black veterans could go on marching as long as –

a: they did it in their own areas;
b: they did it only on Thursday afternoons, which was their time off;
c: they marched only on the rocky patch of veld across the river and behind the blue gum trees. Or in the sanitary lanes, where no one could see them.

Swirsky asked the black ex-servicemen if he could also march with them on Thursday afternoons, maybe drill them a bit, but they said no. They were fine on their own.

My mother said, 'I could have told Nathan Swirsky – East is East and West is West and never the twain shall meet. At least, not till the Last Judgment.'

'What happens then?' my father asked.

'The earth will be consumed with fire and brimstone and the wicked will get boils.'

'Oh, happy days,' said my father.

Gus Trupshaw told Swirsky, 'Hell, it's only natural, isn't it, Natie? I mean, tigers don't mate with bears, do they? The fact is they don't want to be with us. They're happier with their own.'

Swirsky said to us, 'It's the oddest thing, men – the servants wouldn't have me marching with them because I'm a white man! Now, what do you say to that?'

But we didn't know what to say to that.

In the Way

Monk Sava lives in central Serbia, on a forested hillside hard by a river, up a dangerously steep, winding track which he does little to repair. 'Why should I do that?' he asks. 'People will only visit me.'

Each time I travel to ex-Yugoslavia I make a point of visiting Monk Sava. I pretend to be surprised to find him still alive. He pretends to be furious at the disturbance. Each of us is satisfyingly sceptical about the sanity of the other. I think of Monk Sava as the quintessential Serb: he is absolutely certain about all the things he is certain about. These are, in order: the goodness of God; the wickedness of communism; and the destiny of Serbia. He takes the view that Serbs were put on earth to suffer and foreigners were sent to make trouble for them.

He regards me as a peculiar gatecrasher who pitches up on his hillside from time to time. He thinks of me as a German, and as a Catholic. In both of these he is wrong. But neither of us has ever revised our opinions of the other. When I arrive, traditional monastic hospitality requires that he offer me coffee and a spoonful of jam while we reassess each other. But nothing changes.

It's a couple of years since I saw Sava last. In those days you could hear the guns in Bosnia. And in the mountain monasteries of central Serbia, I listened to nuns tell of brothers killed in the fighting. The shooting has stopped – for the moment. In Serbia, 'the late war' is more and more seen as a disaster. Monk Sava believes God visited the war on the Serbs for failing to live according to his word. He traces the disaster back to the long years of communism. Monk Sava was locked up for his religious faith, back in 1957. He calls it doing his time. And now Serbs must live in the bloody aftermath of communist rule. Church, spirit, health, life are spoiled or stolen. There is one consolation: the communists were such virtuosos of catastrophe and ennui that there is nothing left to ruin.

At the back door of Monk Sava's little monastic bunker is a hill that was once a mountain.

If you ask Monk Sava why he moved the mountain, his answer is simple. 'It got in the way.'

The mountain got in the way of his church. To be exact, it also got in the way of a very small graveyard.

Just three wooden crosses tell of the monks who lived here before Monk Sava. But the mountain hemmed them in. Sava does not like being hemmed in. He feels about that mountain with its foot in the graveyard the way he feels about communists – so he got a bulldozer and began to move it. It took a while but now the mountain stands back at a respectful distance and the dead have breathing space.

When the war was at its height in Bosnia its violence even permeated the Church. It was at that time that I spent the Orthodox Easter in the fourteenth-century monastery of Žiča, as the guest of the Bishop. It was here that Serbian kings were crowned. The nuns, who saw their great estates confiscated by Tito's commissars, now keep much to themselves, though they are slightly more visible as the long Lenten season comes to an end and preparations are made for the Orthodox Easter. On Ash Wednesday in the monastery garden a young nun was set to cracking walnuts. She swung her hammer in the late afternoon and the monastery gardens rang with the sound of exploding shards of walnut shells landing amongst the flowers.

On Easter day, after the nettle soup, as the paschal lamb made its way around the table, the Bishop and his friends began to talk and the talk turned to Sarajevo and the war. Not this one, but the one before. In Serbia, wars blur one into the other – sometimes leaping centuries – and so do tales of atrocities. The Bishop remembered how children were orphaned, parents had their eyes gouged out and were hanged by Croatian fascists.

Afterwards, in the monastery garden, the young nun breaking walnuts offered me a challenge: we each took a hard-boiled egg, painted in russet chevrons, and knocked them together. Hers against mine. This old Easter custom is usually accompanied by the greeting: 'Christ is Risen.'

But she told me another version.

'What we say,' she confided as her egg cracked mine with crisp effectiveness, 'is Kill the Mussulman!'

And, later still, when the Bishop heard where I was headed he gave a little perplexed shake of the head. 'That Sava… He does not listen to me. He does as he likes. Not even the mountains does he listen to.'

This time, as I make my uncertain way up the path to Monk Sava's little monastery, winter has relaxed its grip, the trees weep with relief and the mud is terrible. Great black banks of spring ooze, snow melt and leaf-mould make the trek morose. Moreover, there are also signs of a bulldozer. The track is torn; the trees scuffed in passing. Clearly the hermit of the hills had not allowed winter to stand in the way.

I find him halfway up the mountain. Or perhaps it is truer to say the mountain is halfway down towards Monk Sava. He is at the controls of the bulldozer. He leans over the edge of the driver's cab, high above my head, bristling like a furious troll. He also looks surprisingly rakish. He is wearing gumboots into which he has tucked his cassock and a pointed woollen cap. His padded waistcoat guards against the damp and a long, thin, dark blue knitted scarf is wound several times around his throat. His beard is bigger than ever. Naturally, he does not recognize me.

'Who are you?' he yells from his eminence. 'Why have you come here? My monastery's not a cultural monument. It's not even historical.'

The first time we met, he asked, 'Are you a German? I don't like Germans.'

He's in his mid-seventies now. His eyes are perhaps a shade less blue, but his handshake is still pure steel, and he is endlessly at work. For some, temptation comes in the form of sex or money or power. Monk Sava is in thrall to construction. He suffers from masonomania, builder's itch, architectophilia. The monastery must go up; the mountain must come down.

He's right when he says his church has little to recommend it when you compare it with the glories of the Serb monasteries that dot the mountains of these parts. Monk Sava does not much like the celebrated monasteries, he does not much like the hierarchy; he does not much like anyone. He has a horror of the monasteries masquerading as hostels for ambulatory atheists in search of a bit of holy foolishness. For years, under Marshal Tito, the Serbian church had been a lacklustre and largely impotent creature. Tito permitted it to survive at a price crueller than outright suppression, a torment so exquisite only a mischievous genius could have thought of it. He marketed the great monasteries as cultural monuments offering overnight accommodation to inquisitive unbelievers. But the Bosnian war changed all that.

The great monasteries like Studenica or Zica differ from it not just in their splendour but in the very different sorts of priests to be found there. Suddenly the Church became the soul of the nation once more, and, sometimes, an expression of a feverish tribalism.

When Sava wanted a monastery it seemed best he build his own. And without encouragement or funds or help, he began doing so. Monk Sava's temple is small, forgotten, untidy, unfinished. It always will be. And that is what makes the place, like its guardian, so original. The place is a builder's yard, spiky with beams, wire, jumbles of stones and tiles. Junk accumulates and grows into another mountain.

He has a young monk helping him now. And there are also two nuns, tending the kitchen. I watched the young monk disconsolately picking at bits of the hillside where his boss is planning heaven knows what – a parking lot? A heliport? A basilica? I could tell his heart wasn't in it. The hermit's apprentice lacks Monk Sava's gift for tearing into things with hands, feet and teeth. The nuns, Sava allows, have some limited use: they sing the liturgy in church; they prepare coffee and jam for visitors who, however much he tries to discourage them, are constantly turning up to interrupt his building programme.

We walk over to his new, almost built house. It lacks a few details still, but he has lost interest. What is a house when there are hill-sides to move? A young nun of perhaps eighteen, her face carefully averted, serves coffee. We take with our coffee several spoonfuls of strawberry jam and a little plum brandy. Sava is a solitary man but he is well looked after. In fact, he is that rare and paradoxical crea-ture: the well-attended hermit. But he scarcely notices these fellow-labourers in the vineyard. Entirely self-absorbed, like many people at the centre of their own universe, he is, nonetheless, prone to displays of the most alarming modesty.

What, then, I wondered as we finished our coffee, was the earthly solution to the troubles of the Serbs? Given that God's will be done, but it often takes some time.

Sava's blue eyes misted over, his beard grew spiky as a sunflower and his fist crashed down on the table.

'Bring back the King!' cried Monk Sava.

And in the monastery kitchen the nuns fell to twittering and piping like swallows.

Once this challenge would have landed him in jail. He reveres the things that once landed him in jail. He regrets their passing even as he recounts how much he suffered under the old regime, because he knew who he was then, and where in the world he was, and now he has to make a whole new world for himself. Monk Sava is no ordinary rebel – and that was why the last regime had so much trouble with him – he is a Restoration Man. A monarchist calling for the return of the Karageorgevich dynasty. The last King of Yugoslavia was exiled by the communists after the Second World War; the present crown prince, Alexander, was born in a suite at Claridge's in London, which, for the period of his mother's confinement, the Foreign Office declared to be the territory of Yugoslavia.

His voice rises like a cockcrow. 'Oh, look,' he says, 'you're writing all this down. I can expect another spell inside, thanks to you. But let them come and arrest me. You will almost certainly betray me once you get back to Belgrade. You are probably betraying me, right now, with your notebook and your German face and your Catholic faith, but Monk Sava is not afraid. I will take on the communists.'

He slaps me on the shoulder – it is the playful swipe of a tiger's paw. In Monk Sava's laughter I hear a deep, dark note, peculiarly Serbian: something inside him detonates and every bit of him shakes with the force of the internal explosion. And you're left wondering whether to join in, or to duck. Or to call his bluff. After all, no priest has done a spell inside for years, and 'communists' these days hardly admit to the name. Those who might once have locked him up have converted into nationalists, zealots, patriots. Or so they say, but Monk Sava knows better.

He brightens then, and the laugh begins again, somewhere in his toes, and flows up like lava.

'Tell you what,' he says. 'You've never lived under the communists: why don't we give them to you?'

I say I must turn down his gift.

Shaking his head, he says, 'Well, there you are. We poor Serbs, we can't even give them away. Most people in the world are too smart to accept.'

He still cannot get over the fact that I have come specially to see him.

'But why? I am a distinguished nothing. You have interrupted me. Now I must get back to work.'

Since I saw him last he has begun other half-finished projects. Beside the little church the belfry stands uncertainly and I see he has been patching it up; a rickety wooden skeleton supports the bells, but only just. And behind it, between church and belfry, there is parked a very big, very old black Mercedes that Monk Sava keeps to remind himself of the vanities of the world; and the opulence of the Germans, of whom, as a good Serb, he is deeply suspicious; but also as a source of spare parts that may come in useful somewhere, somehow. In Monk Sava's theology, ruination is to be opposed by creation, and a minor home-made monastery is better than holy motels for passing travellers. It is as if his furious labour on the hillside has as its goal the construction of some perfect place. It is also an act of defiance.

Monk Sava knots his scarf, picks up his pointed hat, smooths his beard. Then he kisses me three times with a mixture of bene-dictory grace and relief that I am leaving and as if to pardon my cardinal sins: looking German; being Catholic; and coming all this way to see him.

The last I see of him is a thin man in the cab of the big yellow earthmover, tearing into the mountain at his back door.

The Pink Shoes

On weekdays Alma would come home from work and spread herself emphatically in the basket-weave chair beneath the black-and-white photograph of Leopold Stokowski conducting a symphony orchestra. The orchestra stared dimly at the conductor. The plump solo violinist had settled on the lip of his fiddle a white handkerchief upon which he rested his double chin.

Alma kicked her shoes in a looping trajectory across the room. Pink shoes. High flying, outrageous, like everything about Alma.

Roger usually took up a defensive position in the hooded porter's chair in the corner, placed exactly between the window and the bookcase from where he watched Alma fill the chair and launch her pink shoes into the air, pointing her toes at the ceiling.

He had bought the shoes from the Azerbaijani boutique in the Fulham Road. With their stubby heels and projectile toes, he had known Alma would like them. Their pink was as much a matter of texture as of shade. A hue somewhere delicately between raw veal and exposed human flesh. The pink, though he did not say so, of Alma's tongue. A pink he could taste, veined with a ruddier flush towards toes and heels.

He had told her once that the solo violinist's head, resting on his white handkerchief, reminded him of a suckling pig on a platter.

Alma had pointed out crisply that everything seemed to remind Roger of the farmyard.

Did she mean barnyard?

Alma had shot straight back, 'What's the bloody difference?'

There was, at least in his mind, quite a difference. There were farmyards and there were barnyards. The latter were full of roosters on dung heaps and cocks and hens, cows being led to bulls and stallions serving mares. And at the back of his mind was his mother, years ago, who, finding a packet of condoms in his sock drawer, tapped the gold foil with her forefinger. 'I hope it's never said of you that you preferred the barnyard to basic decency.'

That was exactly what he *wanted.* He wanted it in great muddy chunks. Above all he wanted it with Alma; when she lay back in the basket-weave chair beneath the picture of Stokowski and the suckling pig; when she reached up and played with the painted wooden parakeets swinging from the lamp overhead; when she kicked off her pink shoes and pointed her toes at the ceiling. When she accepted the money he'd given her, an unexpectedly large sum returned to him by the Inland Revenue for an overpayment of tax, saying as she did so that this was something she felt he owed her. When she showed the kind of burliness that knocked people over if they got in her way, people who thought because she was slender and blonde she couldn't knock people over, until they saw her striding away into the distance on her surprisingly strong legs.

He wanted her most when she lifted her legs as she did now in the lamplight. Perfectly circular hollows between ankle and heel. Roger ached to wet the tip of his forefinger and slowly polish the divine hollows of Alma's ankles. Spit would do, or bath water. Oil of evening primrose. Steam. Soap. Baby oil. But all these things required time, leisure, *space*.

People struggled to see Roger and Alma as a couple. Roger, short and dark, pulling slightly at his rather protuberant lower lip. Tall, blonde Alma introducing him with a chopping motion of her right hand. 'Rog. You know Rog.'

People did not know him. When they heard he produced a television programme lasting three minutes, they looked sceptical. *Sounding Off* was a forthright programme and Roger did not seem a forthright man. Alma's friends tended to put him to work. They said, 'Can we leave the drinks to you, Rog?'

He had met her at a party in Camden. Women seemed quite interested when he told them about his job.

'I make people semi-famous for three minutes.'

He had heard these women wondering aloud; had they heard correctly? Roger weighed their hurtful surprise against known advantages of the lure. Among the would-be semi-famous, some ended up on his futon.

Alma hadn't asked him anything that first evening. She told him that she was a 'hunter gatherer'. Only when he spoke of the metaphysics of washing detergents did he realize she must be in advertising. She was at the party with a man called Valentine, a weightlifter, who wore a black body stocking and a red bandana.

46

His muscles rippled with each sip of mineral water. It made Roger queasy. Though why this display of muscularity should so offend him he could not decide. Except he knew there was too much of it.

Later, as he was leaving, Alma stopped him in the hallway.

'Someone said you don't drive.'

Somewhere behind him, Roger heard cheering.

She told him that Valentine had got round to displaying his body.

'Naked?' Roger wondered.

'Valentine wears a posing pouch,' Alma said.

She drove him home in her Japanese sports car, its dashboard bathed in pink/orange light. She spent the night on his futon and never said a word about Valentine the bodybuilder. He remembered how generous she had been. How she had been simply everywhere he reached.

Alma moved in one wet March morning, carrying a tapestry holdall displaying the joys of medieval hunting in a French forest. Royal hunting dogs pursued rabbits with eyes the size of saucers. Alma also carried two plastic bin liners full of shoes. Outside in the street stood a rented van. It took them three hours to transfer all her stuff into the flat. Her books went into his shelves in a haphazard way he did not worry about much at the time, though every so often, in the months that passed, he'd look up and see one of her many paperbacks shouldering aside his collected works of Plato or the Greek tragedians, and feel uneasy at this rough and casual intimacy.

There was less and less space in their Bayswater flat. Alma had a way of spreading herself, a talent for taking over, a fluid imperialism. Alma's mother presented them with a set of Walt Disney's cartoons, very large, and shining, and a flock of wooden parakeets from the jungles of Peru.

Alma had a lot of stuff. He had never had stuff; he lived a stripped and pared life. He'd been on his own a long time, he hated mess, he liked boundaries and yet he realized that something richer, if messier, had come into his world and he told himself he would soon adapt.

She had found a four-poster in a Chelsea loft one day and she had locked his futon in the cupboard. A narrow channel ran down by the wall, his side of the bed, a space close and difficult to move in but which she insisted he use though he bumped his knees. Her side of the bed faced the open room. A map on the wall showed the reefs off the Shetlands.

'I'm ecumenical when it comes to maps!'

And she would lick her finger and stroke the glass as if she could feel the ribbed edges of the reefs, like the armoured plates of some primitive sea monster, lying fathoms deep in the waters off the Shetlands.

From his observation post in the hooded porter's chair, Roger watched Alma undress. She liked to sleep naked, turned on her side, her face towards the luminous view of the radio clock, casting a pink gleam on her hair. Surrounding Alma was what she called her 'air-exclusion area'. And what Roger thought of as his 'no-fly zone'. He turned carefully all night to avoid entering the no-fly zone and lay listening as Alma rhythmically drew in oxygen and gave out carbon dioxide with long, perfect exhalations.

Most people had some capacity to flow. But Roger felt that he was getting nowhere. He was stranded, washed up, a dry stick on a deserted beach. Sometimes he had what amounted to an out-of-body experience. He was floating and looked down and saw thin Roger in bed well outside Alma's air-exclusion area. Roger 'out of the body' would lean down and draw a line around the body of Roger 'in-the-bed', the sort of silhouette you saw drawn in chalk at the site of murders and road accidents to indicate where the body had been, pale evidence of someone who had been there.

Night after night he lay on his side of the big four-poster, the chalk man. He could almost feel himself wasting away. Reduction was his way of keeping sane and keeping his integrity; the less of it he had left, the more possible it became to hang on to it. He reduced his shirts, on their single shelf, from eight to four. He soon owned only two pairs of shoes. He gave his third jacket to an Oxfam shop. And he hung his remaining jackets on a single wire hanger. Standing on Alma's bathroom scales, he saw he had lost weight. He looked in the bathroom mirror, cleared the steam to check, and conceded that he was also losing hair. Each week was a narrow corridor at the end of which stood a closed door. To open that door the slightest crack was his obsession, to slip under it like smoke before it closed again.

He began going through all his books, their books. His classics, Greek and Latin and French, had earned their places on the shelves, and it upset him when he saw Alma knock one over, or pull one off its shelf and then stuff it back. He was always rescuing Cicero or Pliny or Euripides or Montaigne. Each time he would check to see if the book had his name in it and if it did not then he wrote it carefully on the top inside left-hand corner of the front cover. He did not understand why he needed to do this; he knew only that it gave him pleasure and it calmed him.

Each week Roger aimed the arrow of himself towards Saturday night. An hour before Alma awoke on Saturday morning he had set the table for breakfast. Later her bath, first warming her huge fluffy pink towel upon the heated rail, adding just enough bath foam to cover her body as she slipped beneath the water with a sigh and lifted her feet on to the edge of the bath. And then pretending to brush his teeth while watching her in the steamy mirror. If things were destined to go well, he would hear her say, 'Take your toothbrush out of your mouth, Rog.'

He might then coat the tip of his finger with shampoo and slowly polish the circles beneath her ankles while Alma hummed a bit from *Tosca*. Sometimes he forgot to take the toothbrush out of his mouth.

On Saturday nights, in his indecent haste to sleep with her, how often Roger banged his knees in the narrow channel between the wall and the bed while Alma reclined on the soft white hills of her three pillows and looked at him, through him, past him.

'Here I am,' said Roger, and took her hand. 'I'll be up early tomorrow.' Alma removed her hand. 'Tomorrow is Sunday.' He knew he was babbling. 'You can sleep in.'

Her way of seeing through him was especially painful. Other women had seen him and taken to him and held him. He wanted to say that.

She seemed to read his thoughts because she said, rather puzzled, 'Maybe some do. But, frankly, I don't.'

And she got up, superb in her nakedness, went over to the book-case and pulled out a copy of Plato's *Symposium*. He was very angry but he had the feeling before she spoke that she was even more furious with him because she was waving the book over her head.

He wondered if she planned to read the book or throw it. Instead, she opened it, saw his name in the left-hand top corner of the front cover and she screamed. She began yanking out one after the other – Sophocles and Baudelaire and Goethe – shouting his name each time she found it then tossing the books over her shoulder, high, like her shoes, and he lay there watching them sail overhead and crash.

'Why did you do it? Aren't we together? Don't you see what it means? Going around marking your territory?'

He felt he did in a way know what it meant, though he could not have said so for a moment.

For days the books lay about the room like freshly shot birds. And he did not dare, or did not deign – he could not be sure which it was – to pick them up.

A few nights later, Alma was stretched on the sofa, and kicked off her pink shoes which flew high and fell amongst the books. She pointed her bare toes at the ceiling in what was a gesture of angry rebellion and almost as if at a signal the doorbell rang and there in the hall stood Valentine, his sports bag slung around his broad shoulders.

Alma said, 'Hello, stranger. You're in the pink.'

Valentine, it seemed, was working out at the local gym during the day. He was a nightclub bouncer in the evenings. He wore a purple singlet and his muscles still leapt when he sipped his mineral water.

'What's in your bag?' Alma asked.

Valentine told her.

'What's the good of a posing pouch if you don't pose?'

Roger rescued a copy of Virgil from the floor and began reading about the fall of Troy.

Valentine entered the bedroom and came out wearing a tiny triangular patch of black and yellow cloth held up by shoelaces. He got on the table and Alma fetched a bottle of baby oil from the bathroom. Valentine's calf muscle inflated wildly as she rubbed. Neither paid any attention when Roger left the flat.

He arrived home after midnight. He'd not gone more than a few steps in the darkness when he tripped over something and fell down. He lay there for a few moments, aware of the faint lingering smell of baby oil, before getting slowly to his feet and finding the light switch. The pink shoes lay where Alma had kicked them and he had walked into them.

'Lethal,' said Roger.

Alma was sleeping soundly, breathing out carbon dioxide. Roger shook her awake and handed her the tapestry holdall with the fleeing hares and the thin, pursuing hounds.

'Your shoes are in the bag.'

It took her a minute to rub sleep from her eyes. Then she dressed. At the door she said, 'You're doing yourself a bad turn, Roger.'

'Goodbye.'

'You gave me those shoes,' she said.

He sat up all that night in the porter's chair, reading about the fall of Troy. In the morning a moving van arrived. It took a couple of men several hours to carry Alma's stuff from the flat. This was the sort of thing that went on when a government fell and the Prime Minister had to leave his official residence.

The flat was quiet, huge, empty. Roger fetched his futon from the cupboard and threw it on the floor. Lying on his bed, a yellow triangle caught his eye. Valentine's posing pouch. Using Virgil to fish it out of its hiding place under the cupboard, Roger carried the article to the kitchen, pressed tightly between the covers of *The Aeneid*, intending to drop it in the rubbish bin.

But as he passed the bathroom he got lost in all the space Alma had left behind. He felt a bit dizzy. In the bathroom mirror stood a thin man, watching him. Between his paper paws he held a scrap of yellow cotton; its drawstring hung down like the tail of a mouse in the paws of a barnyard cat, like something he had caught and killed.

Whose Zoo

In the early years of Independence, our zoo was lovely. One gatepost was a big wooden chimpanzee, painted chocolate brown, wearing a red fez, supporting on his shoulder the great entrance arch of heavy iron. The other gatepost was a camel cut from yellow sandstone.

Everyone agreed that the animals were happy in our zoo and we were happy too. We knew who we were because we knew where they were. The future looked good.

Then came the Civil War. Government soldiers and rebels bombed each other. The roads were thick with landmines and the fields were full of unexploded ordnance, little round bomblets, rolling like roe from a fat sturgeon. Such was the daily rain of death that we ploughed by night.

The zoo was in a strategic position. It stood on a hill in the capital. Whoever held the zoo held the city; our zoo was taken and lost many times, and each time it changed hands there was less of it.

The soldiers and the rebels did not take – not to begin with at least – the birds and cute tree dwellers: the koalas, the squirrels, as well as the quicker, scrawnier animals they couldn't catch, like the meerkats. They began, sensibly, with food anyone would recognize – zebra, kudu, Egyptian geese and most of the chimps.

And the soldiers didn't eat the zoo all at once, as some say. Of course not. And when there was a sudden run on a species, like the guinea pigs or the okapi, or the big cats, it had no mysterious significance; it was just that soldiers shot up the first cage they came to. Killed, cooked and feasted. They didn't do it for any of the dark reasons, like they craved the strength of the lion in battle, or wished for the audacity of the lynx to enter their hearts. It was a bipartisan thing. Both sides were hungry.

The elephants were next to go. In the beginning there was a kind of hunters' agreement between the two sides: only kill what you can eat. It takes a lot of work to butcher an elephant, and the meat goes off quickly. The sort of ancient hunting agreement that went back to our distant ancestors came into play – kill together, then share the spoils.

But no one, neither rebels nor government soldiers, touched the jaguar – the creamy jaguar from the jungles of South America.

After the elephants, we lost the giraffes, the hippos, the lions and tigers.

And still the jaguar wasn't touched. Quite why he lived wasn't clear. He was lovely, yes, but good looks didn't save the lions from the cooking pot. And the jaguar wasn't even native to our country. Maybe that was it: we've always had a great respect for things from elsewhere. He had this way of moving, slow, like cream uncoiling, like oil on wheels. His eyes were dull from looking through the bars of his cage, but, then, who can blame him? Considering what things he'd seen in our war. Anyway, the troops liked him, and protected him. The soldiers banged the butts of their rifles on the bars of his cage. They called to him: 'Hang in there, man!'

The rebels ate every snake in the place. The government soldiers polished off anteaters, porcupines and mongooses. Then the fighters began working their way down – but the smaller the animal, the more of them it took to make a bellyful. Our zoo was running low in all the cages and, for a while, a kind of rationing came into play: one soldier, one squirrel. The idea being, Hell, we'd better make this stuff last. But generosity dies in wartime and by the time they got to the eagles it was every man for himself.

But no matter how dusty and blasted the zoo got, after the mortars and the strafing, somehow the dreamy jaguar lived on, a little thinner maybe, and he had this habit of muttering to himself and shaking his head, as if he tried every so often to loosen it, even to throw it off.

Then, one day, our government declared the war over, and urged us to vote for national unity. We were reconciled with the rebels and everyone agreed that peace had come to the capital.

That's when we lost the jaguar.

To this day no one knows which side killed, skinned and consumed the jaguar, but a terrible chill fell on us all. Ours had been a family war, a war between brothers and sisters. Once we had a country, and we shot it to pieces. Once we had a zoo, but we went and ate it. Every last thing gone, except for three parakeets. And try as you may, you can't run a zoo on three parakeets – and, anyway, they were balding.

Nonetheless, they might have made it – those parakeets – if

their tail feathers hadn't been green and red. Green and red are our national colours. Peace had broken out, the troops wanted a good time, and some guys simply had to party with red and green feathers in their hair.

Goodbye, war; goodbye, parakeets…

There was nothing left in the zoo now except, sometimes, a faint whiff of elephant; filthy cages, dried camel dung, a little stained straw. It was terrible. The soldiers were dead, the animals gone, but fragile, silly, worthless things survived: orange peel and peanut shells and cigarette ends.

That's when the people began arriving. Queuing at the entrance to the zoo: mothers and their babies, so thin and feverish, flies clustering in their eyes; beggars; and limbless soldiers. The zoo seemed so empty but for many it was a haven. It had water, it had walls, and after the dangers of the countryside, with its thousands of thickly sown mines, it was a safe place.

To begin with there was some discomfort among those of us who lived in real houses. People should not live in the zoo, but, if not there, then where?

And so they came, more and more. Taking over the lions' enclosure and hosing out the polar bears' cage. The seal house was taken by a family of five and in two ticks they had made it as comfortable as could be, with the babies sleeping in the water-trough and washing drying on the bars.

There was, somewhere in our hearts, the nagging question: were things as they should be? It was a source of some embarrassment to us and to our government that others referred to us as the land that ate its zoo. The government said it had been the rebels who did it, and the rebels blamed the government troops. But this could not be allowed to continue since government and rebels were now reconciled, so it was best to agree that no one ate the zoo. Increasingly, it was very hard to find anyone who admitted to having tried the lions or tasted giraffe or roasted a tiger.

The empty birdcages were next to fill with grateful tenants who lived in the enormous soaring aviary. They built nests of corrugated iron in the high corners and widened the niches of the artificial cliff-face where the terns once roosted. The sandy floor of the aviary became home sweet home to your ground-dwellers. Soon there were six families in the split-level development, chattering away like mad, happy as could be.

It's astonishing how many people can pack into a good aviary.

Observers of the zoo dwellers were struck by their inventiveness; how neat, how delicate, how ingenious the truly desperate can be. How they scrubbed and cleaned and fixed themselves a home in the polar-bear den or the lion cage. It was astonishing what they could do with cardboard and tin. Old ammunition boxes grew into bedrooms, the iron casings of cluster bombs were beaten into babies' cradles; and the zoo dwellers did marvels with plastic. Before you knew it they had their new house swept and clean and they were hanging their names on the bars, and calling it home.

Soon there was no more room in the aviary or the giraffes' enclosure or the elephant reserve. The anteaters' den was fully booked, the crocodile ranch and the deer park were filled to bursting.

Down in the crocodile pool several families built from reeds a line of huts, which seemed to float on the water. It was a mixed world: the crocodile families; the polar-bear people; the snake-park settlers...

And still they came – and lived in the stumps of old eucalyptus trees. Grenades had splintered the huge trunks and hungry soldiers had chopped off branches for firewood. Pale trees, the colour of corpses, in a dusty yard, but they were home to some. And our zoo was more full of people than ever it had been of animals.

But, more and more, they came.

The news spread and gawkers turned up wanting to see folk who lived in cages. But gawking turned to disappointment because the people behind the bars looked just like everyone else.

In the zoo itself, a social structure gradually evolved. A pecking order. Families living in reptile cages were seen as cunning and inferior, while people who had replaced lion and buffalo, and who lived on what was called Big Five Hill – the others being elephant, leopard, rhino – were seen as the zoo's natural aristocrats. Social divisions sharpened. Any location above the tiger enclosure was hot property; anything below the crocodile pool was a slum. Added to this was the problem of subletting – there were entrepreneurs who subdivided their cages and rented corners to indigent newcomers at high prices.

Sometimes, in their sleep, ex-soldiers cried out, weeping for the lost jaguar. Or remembering the peacocks. Of course, in broad daylight no one admitted to anything of the sort. They swore that they had never plucked an ostrich, butchered a panther or feasted on flamingo. 'What sort of person shoots falcons?' they said. And they also said, 'Lemur meat has never crossed my lips' and 'I'm proud to say that some of my best friends are lions'.

But questions persisted – what happened to a people who were whispered to have eaten their zoo?

And so, while it was formally announced that no proof had ever been forthcoming that we ate our zoo, our government decided that the only way to stop the rumours, the talk, the speculation was to restore the zoo to its original occupants. It must be said this was seen in some quarters as a retrogressive step as zoos were not what they had been. Many people had doubts. But everyone agreed that only by regularizing our zoological gardens could we put the past behind us and only by facing the question – Whose zoo is it anyway? – could we lay to rest the nightmares of our long and bloody conflict.

And so the clearances began. Of course, those evicted from the cages had to be found suitable alternative accommodation where they might be housed as humans instead of caged like beasts. But it wasn't easy. Some tenants were attached to their cages, and wept as they were led away. Others chained themselves to their bars and chanted, 'Hands off our zoo!' The hippo people picketed the zoo entrance. Tempers flared, and the army had to be called in more than once to restore order.

But eventually the removals were complete and the authorities began restocking our zoo. Back they came to their cages, the elephants, the lions and tigers, the seals and the polar bears. The zoo was restored, right down to the metal arch carried by the sandstone camel and wooden chimp – and everything was as it had been.

And yet the funny thing was that when the cage dwellers were removed, we felt we had lost something. Something valuable. Those settlers, those inmates, had been so inventive, so happy. They'd coped, they'd thrived, they'd shown a knack for captivity – they'd painted their bars, swept the floors, slung hammocks and raised children in spaces so small you couldn't swing a cat in them.

But it could not go on; people were simply not made to live in the zoo. Because if they stayed then who were they? And who were we? Oh, yes, it was very good to have everything back where it was supposed to be. We admired the armadillo and the polar bear; we welcomed home the musk deer and the creamy, dreamy jaguar from the jungles of South America. Even if they did not seem altogether happy to be back.

We said to ourselves, 'Well, they'll be happy soon enough, won't they?' We looked into the eyes of the okapi and the bongo and we whispered, 'Well, if not you, then who?'

The Day Out

Damian sang as he drove. Under a violet sky which even the ozone filters in the anti-sun roof of his car could not sully, Damian filled his single lung with filtered air and sang his heart out.

To his left was a field of geep, their heads swivelling to watch him pass, their tails lifting as they turned. Identikit animals mutated for lower fat and more flavour. Damian dimly remembered the fashions of his youth, when men and women had worn a similar single yellow ring through their ear lobes.

Great and many, as they liked to say on the late-night simulcasts devoted to the triumphs of science, great and many were the reasons why Damian should not have felt like singing. There was the endless, unstoppable rise of the rouble to which all major currencies were helplessly captive. The defection of the prime minister to China, though not unexpected, had been made worse by her statement that this was what her grandmother would have done but for misguided loyalty to her party, and her party had repaid her loyalty by dumping her. There was the tendency of the old king to weep in public whenever one of his trees died. The Caliphate's siege of Belgrade had entered its twentieth year.

But Damian sang even so as the car carried him through the countryside and the transponders buried in the road corrected his direction in a series of gentle shudders. This was his day out. The face he saw in his rear-view video was round, full, relaxed. To anyone detaining him, if they did not demand to read his carbon-dating ring, he could have passed for a man in early middle age. In fact, he was ninety years old, follicularly sound, with a flesh-to-bone ratio that many would kill for. True, he was one airbag short of full safety standards – but you could not see his missing lung and it still was external imperfections only that were jeered at in the streets.

Only that morning the simulcast had told of a woman who coughed on the Maglev and was thrown from the car by furious passengers. Yet a politician who lied about his cerebral implant might well have kept his job had he not been spotted by a team of head scanners on a surprise inspection.

Damian had lost his lung back in the old days, during the Warming. It had happened in Brighton, when a plant turning out memory chips had polluted the air and many had sickened. The plant, naturally, had been neutroned and the resultant destruction shown on neighbourhood notice-boards and laptops across the planet. But that had been a long time ago. The pictures had faded from the screens and now Brighton lay like Atlantis beneath the warm sea.

As a result of the accident Damian had found himself, at twenty, unemployable. So, after taking a three-day course at the television centre, Damian had been despatched as a cost estimator to a Theatre of Deprivation.

There were many of these failed states, run by the Health and Security Authorities. Damian was despatched to Middle Land, a crescent stretching thousands of kilometres from coast to coast, depopulated by the viral epidemics. He travelled by armoured train, attended by the usual staff, calculating the amount of maize permitted per head, building airfields for the food drops. Cooped up in the control room, staring at the reports beamed in from closed-circuit cameras in devastated villages, he suffered continually from the cost estimator's usual aches and pains, especially monitor's neck.

The frontier was tough and the people starving in the villages were ungrateful. Official videos beamed into those villages by the protection forces made it clear that it was only by staying there that some, at least, would survive the shortages. His train once struck and killed several indigenes fleeing their villages. It seemed to Damian that they preferred to die beneath his wheels but, of course, it would have been quite incorrect to have said so. And Damian valued his job.

Ruby-May co-ordinated the succour run, the immense airborne food trains droning out of China heavy with grain and drugs and administrators for the imploded countries. He liked Ruby-May and she liked him. So they made an agreement.

When they returned from the Theatres of Deprivation, and began living together, people were, quite naturally, suspicious. Ruby-May had been out in the Theatres for a long time. Who could say what she might be carrying? Ruby-May had been very understanding about this and took to heart their very real concerns, even though every test showed her to be clean. But even so she always wore her hypoallergenic gloves whenever she left the house and she was happy to retreat into the sterile bubble whenever friends came to dinner. It did little good to tell people that she'd been screened on her return from the other world and shown to be acceptable. Nowadays, people were immensely virally aware. You simply felt you had to support their right to personal anxiety, even if science said you were as clean as a whistle.

Then quite without warning, as was the way, her GP appeared on the screen one night to say he'd had a call from the Genealogical Office. It seemed that Ruby-May's maternal background showed unacceptable risk. He strongly advised a pre-emptive strike. Ruby-May cried and said she wouldn't do it. But the firm young face on the screen reminded her that if she chose to ignore the figures, and the disease struck, she might be refused treatment in much the way, long ago, smokers, drinkers, cholesterol addicts, the overweight, the undersized and those found to carry the gene for violence were routinely turned aside as being deemed to have brought their misfortunes upon themselves.

So Ruby-May had pre-emptive breast surgery and all had been fine for about ten years when her GP reminded her that she was now over seventy and that every succeeding year her chances of being struck by the family probability increased markedly. Better safe than sorry. Leave it too long and it could be dicey.

So Ruby-May decided to have the other breast removed.

And that should have been that. But a few days later the mail box bleeped and postal announcements told Ruby-May her GP had something he wanted to share with her.

The face on the screen was as smooth and as white as one of those ancient clock faces you sometimes saw in very old videos of very old churches before they all fell down. The General Gene Practitioner had looked at her LEG rating. Ruby-May was, of course, free to ask what her cut-off prediction was. She was a little over seventy and the average Life Expectancy Grade for a woman was about 136. Men still trailed at about 125. No one knew why, though the latest best guess in the clinic was that it related to falling sperm count. Ruby-May said, after much reflection, that she did not want to know her LEG, because they only ever revised these things downwards.

'Say I am to go at a little more than a hundred, or even younger – at ninety-something. Do I want to know? Damian, I do not.'

One day Damian came home to find his dinner in the microwave and a note from Ruby-May:

Heat on Mark 5 for 30 seconds. Have taken the day out.
Love R-M
P.S. Do not over-cook

That had been nearly twenty years ago. Now he was on his day out. He needed the break. But he couldn't remember why he needed a break. He'd tried every enhancer on the market. But his memory grew worse. He kept his forgetfulness to himself. He signed up to one of the biggest memory banks on offer. He never strayed without a connective device so he could access the facts he needed – in case someone asked him something he couldn't remember.

It was so bad he could not even remember when they had shot the poets. He could remember what the poets had said before they shot them – that they were copywriters, or underwriters, or ships' writers or public relations people of vestigial account who had never harmed anybody. But it hadn't helped – they shot them. And Damian could not remember why.

Damian was happy because he had made up his mind – this was his day out, his away day, and his choice.

The perfect fields slid by like well-made beds. To his left, glasshouses scarlet with non-bruising tomatoes. To his right, fields full of impervious cabbages, made safe from pests by their genetic slices of scorpion poison. Never had more people been so healthy or lived longer. Yet there seemed no way of solving the inherent contradiction: the more health precautions you enforced, the more ills attacked the human frame.

When his vehicle suddenly slowed he thought he must have lost power for some reason. It was only when the window opened and a squeaky voice demanded to know why it had been picking up oscillations in the vehicle that Damian realized that he might be in some trouble.

'I was singing,' he said carefully.

That the police officer found this unsatisfactory was clear from the twinkling line of lights that glowed between its plastic brows. Police officers' voices were designed to deter. This one sounded like he'd OD'd on nitrous oxide.

'Please end unnecessary vocal oscillations within the vehicle.'

'Yes, Officer.'

The cop began checking the vehicle's instruments, voice recorder, alcohol monitor, anti-nicotine screener, adiposity gauge. Then it read off the destinations on the navigational computer.

Looking at the officer buzzing and flashing, Damian caught

himself thinking 'LMSB…' and immediately felt ashamed of this petty computerism. 'Large memory, small brain' was an old gibe which really didn't stand scrutiny any longer: the new officials had a considerably improved brain function. It was an offence to suggest, even by demeanour, that electronic officials were any less worthy of respect than carbon-based beings.

The cop now looked Damian over. Its grey glassy protruding eyes were icy.

'Where are you heading?'

'To the day centre. I've decided to take a day out.'

'Why have you loaded your smart card with only enough credit for a one-way trip? Single trips, to whatever destination, are forbidden. To deliberately set out on a journey without sufficient credit to return is an offence.'

Though it was always useless to argue, Damian said he felt sure that there were exceptions. A day out, for instance.

The officer saluted, fined him and withdrew in one smooth action.

'There are no exceptions. An appropriate penalty has been deducted from your account. You may proceed.'

The first he saw of the day centre was a strawberry neon sign on the roof. CAMP SUNRISE WELCOMES ONE AND ALL. He imagined a simple, pleasant little ceremony. The couch, a cup of tea and a biscuit, a smile from the nurse, the slight discomfort of the needle, and away you went.

That's how he had always thought of Ruby-May's day out. Telling the nurse cheerfully that she was 'genetically privileged' and how she had lost one breast and then the other because that's what her genotype said she should do. Ah, yes. Ruby-May had been the closest thing he knew to an old-fashioned patriot. Ruby-May had played it by the book. My genotype, right or wrong. If pre-emptive surgery was indicated, then that is what you had done. But she wasn't going to wait around until they'd removed everything that made her who she was. He understood and admired her for that.

He had to wait for many hours. There was a long line of away-dayers ahead of him and it was nightfall before he got inside the centre. A revolving workstation in a striped apron was hosing out a giant fridge. It was evidently one of those dual jobs, an operator programmed for cleaning and consolation. It depended for readings on its sensitive sniffer and, coming close, it nuzzled him gently, like a dog, testing whether he was organic. Identifying him from his breath as 'human, elderly, one lung only, slight liver damage', it switched to consolatory mode.

'Go home, my son,' it advised, in warm brown vowels. 'Thank you for your understanding. We're closing down now.' Then it fitted a nozzle into its mouth and began sucking ash out of the ovens.

Damian was bewildered. He sat down at an empty table on which someone had left a pile of glasses and a dozen unopened beers. A geranium wilted in a pink plastic tub. Remnants of some happy family's day out. Damian had been glad, when he'd set off that morning, that he had no one to see him off. Days out were not about those who had gone but those who remained. And they could be wild. The aim was sustainable mourning but it did not always work that way. Once guests were high on their opiates of choice they would offer 'a cheer and a tear for the near and dear', though by now few remembered why they were there. Keening and rending then followed and this sometimes saw mourners pitted against one another in spectacular displays of competitive grief.

The workstation rolled towards him and breathed in his ear, softly, kindly. 'We can't have you today. No, we can't. Thank you for your patience. This is a day centre, and you are here after dark. Goodnight and safe home.'

'But this is my day out,' he told the machine.

'Days out and all away days must take place according to the general rota. Unless you're private. Are you private?'

Damian said he was not private.

'Get yourself a private scheme, my son,' said the workstation. It finished stacking syringes in a sterilizer and began sealing the drug cabinets. 'Save yourself a lot of grief.'

'But I thought you just turned up for your day out. I thought everyone was allowed?'

The workstation hummed to itself, a low, perplexed meditation as it polished the doors of the great ovens. When it spoke again its voice had shifted from consoler to irascible official. Where, it asked, had Damian been living for the past few decades? Camp Sunrise took emergencies only. There were waiting lists. To get an early day out you had to prove sufficient need. Stretcher cases took priority. And there were delays. Jams in the fridges; dust damage in the ovens. In theory you got an away day when you wished but the practice was not like that. The machines were old. They needed investment. The authorities preferred to target specific groups. Groups in need. The workstation reverted to consolation. 'The Management of Cape Sunrise thanks all Day-Outers for their understanding and apologizes for any inconvenience.'

70

'Tomorrow – can I try again tomorrow?' Damian asked.

'Tomorrow,' said the workstation, 'is taken.'

The door opened, a long finger of light pointed him into the dark.

Damian stood in the dark. All his tomorrows stretched ahead – as far into the future as he could see. Except he could see nothing. Where, when was his day out? He'd always believed in a decent conclusion. You might not be able to prevent it but you could smooth it over, organize it properly and fairly. That was what all science showed. A friendly finish. But now the end began to look as if it hadn't even begun.

Wall Story

Chi-Chi's harks back to those watering holes that once you would have found all over town until no one went out at night to anywhere that wasn't a shopping mall. Chi-Chi's bar is so passé it sometimes seems like a film set. The traffic growls past the front door, the specials are chalked on a blackboard on the pavement, a notice over the door says 'No weapons' and the hotel rooms above the bar are not really hotel rooms at all, but niches and nooks where the girls from the avenue take their clients.

Chi-Chi is a Portuguese from the old Lourenço Marques and he drinks with his customers, mostly salesmen in soap and shoes and windscreens. He likes stories; he likes holding the floor. Sometimes a guy will put his head round the door of the bar and say, 'Where is Diane?' And Chi-Chi, without looking up, will say, 'Room 22 – but she's in a meeting.'

One night he told us about the wall.

'Hey, what about these guys building the biggest wall in town? Seven bloody k's it'll be. It'll wrap around the whole of Hyde Park. This baby is so *ginormous* it will run from Sandton Drive to William Nicol Highway and Rivonia. A mix of metal and chain mail and razor wire that'll claw the fucking skin off anyone who so much as touches it. And above the razor wire, you got half a metre high electric fencing. And the juice in the electric wires is hot enough fry the balls off any fucker who chances his arm. And there'll be sensors under the wall that trigger alarms in the sentry boxes. And cameras... fifty of these bitches strung along the wire. Not even a fly will piss without those cameras picking it up and phoning home to mother with the pics. What's more, there'll be two armed-response vehicles, Humvees, specially imported from the States, with guards riding the wire day and bloody night, packing pump-action shotguns. It doesn't come cheap either. Gonna cost those bozos five thousand bucks – that's a lot to cough up each cal month... But I guess they don't think of the end of the cal month, those bozos. They're so fucking loaded. But there's nothing better than a good wall, hey?'

Everybody likes a good wall. It speaks of security, of how things are.

There is a big guy at the end of the bar, drinking cane and Coke, and he speaks for everyone when he says, 'You can't have too much wall. The bozos who come by night, they'll lift your electronic gates clear off the hinges – while the CCTV looks on! A good high wall with lots of stuffing fizzing though the razor wire cuts down on that.'

Chi-Chi thinks for a bit and then says, 'I'll tell you something walls also cut right down on, *ou maat.*'

'What's that?' says the cane drinker.

'Fooling about.'

'Come again?' says the big guy.

'Serious. I bullshit you not. You guys read about the White Mouse case? Weird! There's this guy called Dr Ferreira, he's single and he teaches something airy-fairy at the university. This Ferreira lives over Parkview way, next door to a guy called Mickey Michau and his wife, Marianne. They live in two old houses that haven't been done. Know what I mean? Low walls, low wooden gates, left over from way back when. Like you used to get them back in the fifties, I guess. Fuck-all security. No alarm, no razor wire, no nothing. And the Michaus and this Doc Ferreira, they're big buddies, they talk over the garden fence, they walk into each other's houses any time, they don't lock the doors.'

'I know what you're going to say – they get wiped out. Another cane. Make it a double,' says the big guy.

Chi-Chi doesn't stop talking as he fixes the drink. 'Michau's a rep, right? He travels in soap – all over the country, Durban, Cape Town, etcetera. Regular hours. But this Ferreira guy, he's doing his airy-fairy thing at the varsity, so he doesn't work regular hours, and he's at home a lot and he drinks coffee with Marianne, who doesn't work at all, right? And it's great. Then one day Mickey Michau comes back from Angola, like a day earlier than he's expected because – surprise, surprise – Angolan phones don't work half the bloody time, and he hasn't told Marianne. But so what? He knows she'll be pleased. He pulls up outside the house … and parks.'

The big guy says, 'Sheez – no garage even?'

Chi-Chi grins. 'I told you. No nothing. You with me? Ferreira

74

and Michau always park in the street. How they kept their cars I don't know. Anyway, Michau opens the garden gate and he can see the light on in the bedroom because the Ferreiras and the Michaus have these bedrooms which you can see into, and what he sees is two people in the window, and one of them is his wife and the other is a man who doesn't have many clothes on. So what to do? Well, what Ferreira does is he puts down his brief-case, and he creeps…' Chi-Chi leans his elbows on the bar counter and mimes a leopard crawl '… across the lawn till he's right under the window. He gets right under the bedroom window which is open because Mickey and Marianne, they like to feel the night air on their faces. So they sleep with their windows open! And through the window Mickey hears his wife and she is making these squeaks, like a white mouse, over and over. Eek! Eek!

'So what does he do? He goes round to the front door – he doesn't need his keys, because the Michaus are the sort of people who don't ever lock their front doors – and he walks into the house and he doesn't bother to walk quietly. When he gets into the bedroom it's empty, and the bed is a bit messed. He walks around the room wondering where everybody is. He gets to the cupboard, he opens it and there is Marianne, and she's totally nude, except for her cellphone, which she's holding in her right hand. And Michau looks at her and he says, "Hello, Old Mother Hubbard in the cupboard. Where's the white rat?"'

'Well, it turned out that Doc Ferreira, when he hears Mickey stomping up the passage, has jumped out of the window, and he's back home by now.'

'You're bullshitting us,' said the big guy.

Chi-Chi's thrilled. 'I swear to God it's true. I read it in the papers. They were in court for the divorce, Dr Ferreira and the Michaus. Only maybe they didn't like the rat bit 'cause they called it "the white mouse case". It's weird, hey? Most houses got a wall. Think about it. There are still white mice who live like that.'

We thought about it. It was more than a story – it was a kind of fairy-tale about a house with no wall.

Anywhere else it would have been love, passion, adultery that counted, and got written and sung about. Not in Jo'burg. It wasn't a story about those things. It wasn't sexy, it wasn't funny – it was weird. It was hard for us to think about Marianne's squeaks of passion, of two naked bodies in a bed, of Marianne in the cupboard holding a cellphone.

Here were two families who were living in the twenty-first century just as people had lived back in the distant 1950s, when you met and mixed with your neighbours, little boys climbed trees in the next-door orchard, and women drove alone at night. When people slept with their windows open because they liked feeling the wind in their faces.

The guys at the bar leaned back, they lifted their noses and sniffed the night air, like Mickey Michau had done. They breathed in the freedom of being alone in your own garden, a time when a man could do the leopard crawl, one elbow after the other, across his own patch of lawn, up to his bedroom window, which stood wide open, and listen to his wife squeaking in the African night… 'Eek! Eek!'

Covered Bridge and Autumn Splendour

It began when he moved into the flat overhead. Without warning, the windowpanes began to tremble and dust fell from the ceiling.

Miranda knew all about him. 'That's Boris. He makes music.'

I've always thought this was an unhelpful way of putting things. Why not 'He makes mud pies?' 'He makes tortellini?' Or 'He makes hay while the sun shines?' I'd say, frankly, that stroking the contrabass is an offensive act. If more people were exposed to its booming voice, operators would need a licence.

Miranda said, 'Listen to his sarabande. Don't you love his gigue?'

But I could not tell one from the other. All I heard was a wooden boom like upstairs thunder.

Normally, I wouldn't have minded. This is Maida Vale and you get all sorts. If there are any back-street abortionists left, this is where they're hiding out. These big houses have lofty airs, bold exteriors and bits of stucco: a grimy grandeur. But inside there is a warren of flimsy partitions, and sounds travel easily. We are used to sex and screams. Whole lives are broadcast nightly on the domestic airwaves. What goes on behind the curtains would make a sailor blush.

Here, estate agents are soothing counsellors. When the gentleman banker was deliberately run over in the road opposite, word was not to worry – he hadn't been around long enough to affect property values.

And after dark the ambulance sirens begin. Some nights are like one long air-raid. To which harbours of pain they're headed no one knows, but they all seem to leave from here.

The man before the bassist had been something in polymers and Miranda had been somewhat unexpectedly gripped by what might have seemed to some, though not to me, an odd but rather amusing interest in plastics. Perhaps it was in her nature to be compulsively drawn to someone or something that I was not. I think of her as alarmingly susceptible. I'd find her reading things like *Plastics and Polymers: A Celebration* in what I can only describe as a spirit of mute rebellion.

She did not share my interest in maps.

'Maps are dull, flat, boring,' she said.

In fact, looked at the right way, maps are teeming with interest, and their great advantage, if you prefer, as I do, contour maps, is that they say very little about people. And that is a considerable relief.

Added to what I began to think of as the echo in the attic, the aching basso profundo upstairs, I had to hear Miranda telling me that Boris also read music, as if this was something miraculous. I

78

said I did not mind him reading music, if only he would not go on to translate what he read into the groaning dirge above my head. I understood that the notation on the page encouraged the musician to turn it into sound but, frankly, I would have preferred it if he didn't do so.

Miranda said, 'But that's how you get into the music. You drown in it. Risk your life in it.'

That is a terrible idea. I like very much indeed the depiction of rivers and mountains and oceans on maps of countries I do not know. I can look at them for hours. But I do not wish to walk in the Himalayas or see the Irrawaddy flowing through my living room. The last thing I want to do is to swim in it. And I am never tempted to inflict my interests on my neighbours.

'Why don't you just listen?' Miranda asked. She didn't seem to know she was shouting.

And as if he had heard her, Boris began touching and plucking the strings of his bass, which meant, I had learnt, that he was tuning it. I did try listening, but all I heard was heavy furniture scraping across bare floorboards. Or dairy cows groaning to be relieved of their milky burden. But, then, I'm not musical.

'I wouldn't trust you to hum,' said Miranda, with that little gunslinger's pout and a sharp puff of air, as if she was about to blow smoke off the barrel of her six-shooter.

One evening Boris asked us up for a drink, which Miranda said was kind – considering how hard he worked. She said we should be very quiet on the stairs and I said, categorically, that I refused to tiptoe.

Boris wore dungarees, his beard was white and he was carrying a long slightly droopy stick, which he waved like a wand.

'Boris has a French bow,' said Miranda. Like Boris had X-ray eyes, or wings of purest gold.

First thing I saw, filling his flat, was the double bass. Leaning against the wall.

Miranda gave Boris this little fluttery eyelash look that said, God, I'm *dying* of embarrassment. Ignore my husband – he's so unmusical.

Boris smiled, *loudly*, in Canadian fashion, with depressingly good teeth. I knew that he ate red meat.

Varnish, said Boris, was the secret of a good fiddle. All the best old Italian fiddle makers knew their varnish.

Not only did Boris have a French bow, but his instrument was Italian and historic. And if it was fat, voluptuous, darkly curved and gleaming, then that meant fat was good for you, like it was good for Sumo wrestlers.

The bass leaned against the wall the way bloated men once leaned against street corners in silent movies; picking their teeth and gut-butting passers-by.

Boris had painted his flat igloo-white because, he told Miranda, colour interfered with his concentration. We stood around the bass like it was a prize bull and Miranda said it was really much bigger than she had thought and leaned forward and stroked the strings. The thing groaned and she laughed; then we all laughed. Boris said he'd been practising so he'd just go and wash the rosin from his fingers.

And then Miranda told me that rosin was the stuff fiddlers rub on their bows.

'You get it from pines.'

I don't know why this sort of information can be so alarming.

'You get it from pines.' Why does a grown woman go around saying things like that? I have never been more disgusted in my life. Well, actually I have – that time Miranda fell for the man who owned a plastics factory, and she talked of nothing but polymers for weeks and swore that if she had her time again she would study chemistry because synthetics were the way of the future.

Miranda is, *was*, a publisher's editor and her business is words on the page, and she loves it, though she says it ruins you for reading. You're always seeing the mistakes. I work in the City where I calculate the imaginary rise and fall of arcane financial instruments, and when I think of a winner I stick a few quid on it. It's a kind of fiscal bingo, but it pays, and our flat is large, though porous. In my spare time I have my maps. The point about cartography, from the point of view of an interested observer, is that you never have to go to the places they represent, but you do have a very exact knowledge of how to get there, should the need arise, and which I have always hoped would not happen.

I worry about susceptibilities, and I have said so to Miranda. When I first met her, all she owned was a futon and a lot of books and she's always been semi-vegetarian. But soon after the arrival of Boris upstairs, Miranda began to eat meat. *Lots* of meat.

What time Boris did not devote to carnivore delights he spent practising, and for much of the afternoon our ceiling would vibrate and soon Miranda was coming home early just to hear him. And she became missionary about meat. As often as not when I got back from the office she'd be grilling a huge steak. She'd throw it on the griddle, weigh it down with an old flatiron, singe it and then devour it. While upstairs it was milking time and the loudly lowing herd would be winding slowly across my ceiling...

This before seven of an evening! And all the while the music upstairs poured out. Molten. That's the thing about the low notes of the bass: they get inside you, like woodworm. They shake you until you feel yourself falling in. And your wife sits at the table devouring a side of beef.

'I'm ravenous,' said Miranda.

When Boris had first come to London, he had had to buy a second seat on the plane, just for his bass. Miranda's tone suggested that this journey ranked with the Kon-Tiki expedition, or a moon landing. Boris and his bass, flying to London. Boris was forever going on about his home town, Halifax, and the beauties of Nova Scotia.

'Boris', said Miranda, 'yearns for Halifax.'

When they got on to the subject of Canada, I preferred not to listen. But like the bass notes, the news got inside me somehow. Miranda told me about it the way she once told me about plastics. Along with music and meat, my life was now crammed with salient details about the Maritime Provinces. It is painful to be given non-stop history lessons in bed.

Did I know that years ago there'd been a great explosion in Halifax harbour? A French ship stuffed with high explosives caught fire and blew up. Most of the town was destroyed and hundreds died. Bunches of keys were welded together by the heat. There wasn't a bigger bang on earth till Hiroshima.

Did I know that Halifax sent the ships that pulled people out of the sea when the *Titanic* went down? There is a museum in Halifax where the surviving deckchairs are displayed in a glass case. Above all, Halifax is a bright and sparkling port; and Nova Scotia is packed with forests, lakes and wandering moose.

And all the time Miranda was talking, above our heads the bass wept and mooed.

One evening I got home and I was not met by the smell of steak. The flat was empty and horribly quiet. No cows. Just Miranda's note.

It was a classic of its kind. 'What can I say? Don't take it personally.'

It's odd how bits of information about Maritime Canada may, if used in the right way, become a great tranquillizer. Think of the Halifax explosion. The force of the blast was so great that every drop of water in the harbour evaporated. For a few seconds, there was just this dry hole where the sea had been.

I know how that feels.

Boris and Miranda took a flat, not very far away, I believe. But, then, Maida Vale is full of lost corners where no one goes. A few streets left or right, and you can vanish.

I moved too. Not far, but far enough. I still know nothing about the gigue or the sarabande. I do know rosin comes from pines. I feel nothing for plastics.

For some time I've been posting Miranda a series of picture postcards. My notes are brief but fervent. I'm an enthusiast, a patriot. Anyone reading my cards would know I have settled very happily in Nova Scotia and I am at home in Halifax.

It's all perfectly genuine. The cards are, anyway. They're printed in Canada. They show the usual tourist stops: the deckchairs from the *Titanic*; the band in the public gardens; pine forests – oh, and plenty of moose. I address the cards and send them to Halifax, then this agency stamps and mails them to Miranda's office in London.

Boris and Miranda hear from me regularly. This week I posted a real beauty. It's called 'Covered Bridge and Autumn Splendour'. An old bridge shouldering its snug timber canopy, painted red and thick with late summer flowers. The colours are awful, actually, but it is heart-rending propaganda designed to move the expatriate to a frenzy of nostalgia. Nostalgia you'd want to drown in. Yearning you'd wish to lose your life in.

At least, that is my fervent hope because Boris can yearn all he likes, but he can't go back because he knows I'm there and I've made it more my place than it ever was his. Halifax is home and I show it to be so, each week at least. I've colonized it.

Then there are the three air tickets he'd have to fork out for, if you count Miranda. Let him eat his heart out in Maida Vale.

I've also taken up the violin. Well, Irish fiddle, actually. The clubs of Halifax (how easily now I find my way around the place) from the waterfront to the Citadel, are full of singers who sound as if they come from Ireland. Sometimes I send Miranda recordings of migrant songs, lost-at-sea songs, love songs – anything that hurts, really.

I scratch away at the fiddle of an evening. I'd never claim to be making music, and sometimes the girl who lives below me will drop in. I rub my bow, which is not French, with rosin and I do not tell her it comes from pines. I don't tell her, either, that what I play is Canadian folk trying to be Celtic. Her great love is Western music and I don't want to hurt her. She's Chinese. That's OK. Maida Vale is full of foreigners. Like me.

How It Was

Shadows clung to the outlines of Siggie's stories, dark as stubble on an ogre's jaw.

'Poor Sandrine! Wearing a blue nightdress. With pink roses – pink, over the breasts. And a midnight-blue dressing-gown, tied with a silvery cord. And Turkish slippers.'

Siggie tells the story of Sandrine in the moonlight and her husband Nimmo to anyone who will listen and he tells it in a matter-of-fact tone. And so he should. It is true. I have seen the barn, inspected the damage. I have talked to everyone involved, except Sandrine. I met Nimmo when he offered his fire-damaged clocks to an antique shop, over in the Massif Central, not far from Roquefort. I've met his friends, the ones he was drinking with at the *Miel du Midi* the night Sandrine waited for him in the garden. They are a gendarme, a hunchback and Siggie, the clockmaker.

Let Siggie begin telling the story and I've noticed how his clients, like Vim, the Dutch banker who buys his clocks, and Hans, the German doctor who collects oil lamps, and Theo, the computer man, purse their lips as if they were longing to wash his mouth out with soap. They think these tales exhibit juvenile bad taste, like spitting in public or worshipping idols. They hate the expansiveness of Siggie's stories, their wondrous elements and his childlike belief in luck. It is not that he is religious – it is worse than that – he regards as natural and ever-present the world of magic and miraculous good fortune. His mind is that of a man who grew up reading the Brothers Grimm and had never seen the world differently.

They listen and they ask how can he know exactly what Sandrine wore on that terrible night? Sandrine in the moonlight that burns silver, quick and dangerous as a viper, with her little box of matches? Who told him? Or did he make it up? What right has he got to tell us what she was thinking as she stood there in the driveway outside her house, waiting for husband to come home? In a world where only oil and accountancy are real, what is this stuff supposed to be about? That is the question Vim and the others constantly think but do not ask out loud.

I happen to know that Vim drinks and punches his wife and yet he qualifies as grown-up. I watch the small vein pulsing in his broad temple when Siggie begins. I see the look of impatience and then fury. I see, too, how cross he gets because Siggie, so delighted with the tale he's told many times, has no idea that Vim thinks him not just crazy but somehow disgraceful and a liar.

Siggie has no interest in lying but he is susceptible to enchantment, he wants to pierce the mystery of why a woman who has been married for many years suddenly one night tried to destroy her husband and everything he owned. He tells people about

Sandrine because he believes the story points towards the only thing he does believe in. The mystery – if only he could understand how it worked – is not about magic, it's about riches. He might seem to some as if he stepped out of a fairy-tale but if he has, his interest is the same as that of Rumpelstiltskin – it is not folklore, it is finance that he is after. Turning straw into something more valuable than horse feed – that is his dream. He tells the story not because he makes it up but precisely because he could not make it up and no matter how many time he tells it he still cannot believe it.

That's the thing. You grow up, join a bank, beat your wife, live in the adult world and that is fine. But when someone tells you quite seriously that there was once a very small man with a soft smile, and a gentle manner whose wife liked physics and one night set out to kill him you accuse the witness of telling stories.

Siggie says helplessly, faced by the mystery of that night, 'That's how it was.'

Sandrine has gone now and so has the house. All we have left to go on is Nimmo and I don't think he has a clue why she did it. Nimmo is over seventy, a frail person, with a scattering of silver hair and tiny hands which he rubs together when he thinks of Sandrine. He started as a rag-and-bone man, a collector of scrap, and he parlayed his daily collection of junk into a fortune. His big chateau in the hills above Mazamet in the Tarn has a long driveway and on the gateposts stretch great white marble lions, their sleeping heads colossal on their paws. His money went to buy old aeroplanes, vintage cars and grandfather clocks.

On Friday nights Nimmo visited the *Miel du Midi* – a bar at the top of a flight of stairs, in the loft of an old tannery in Mazamet. He drank there with Hercule, the hunchback, Jules, the gendarme, and Siggie, the clockmaker. Hercule always reminds me of an amiable artichoke – it is his wedge shape and the ribbed quality of his build. Jules, the policeman, by contrast, is dark, tall and tanned. Siggie invariably wears a tweed sports coat with leather buttons and combs his long grey hair in a series of loops that follow the lines of his broad forehead, to which it is plastered with some sort of pomade that smells of musk and verbena.

These four had a ritual. They would drink in the bar until 11, after which Nimmo would step into his car. Always a punctual man, he'd arrive home at 11.15 and drive his car into the vast barn where he keeps his vintage cars and planes – three old Porsches, a pair of Mercs, a Tiger Moth and a Messerschmitt.

Nimmo told Siggie, 'I knew how it was with her, that night, when she waited in the garden for me to come home…'

'How could you know?' Siggie wondered.

Nimmo shrugged. 'One knows, that's all. When something like this happens to you – afterwards, you know why it happened. It's like a secret whispered in your third ear.'

'Seen by your third eye,' said Siggie.

'Ear,' said Nimmo. 'She saw things that never were and she heard things that weren't there either. She saw me in places where I never was. She had visions, very good ones. She described very well the *boîte* where she saw us carousing every Friday night. A palace of pleasure. With black bouncers on the door. Fountains of flowing champagne. Or was it sherbet? And afterwards… she saw me going upstairs to bed with young girls. It sounded good, I wanted to be there. Only… there was no there in which to be.'

'There is no upstairs in that bar,' Siggie said.

There is no downstairs either. There is a single floor, with the bar at one end. There are sometimes, on Friday nights, a clock-maker, a gendarme and hunchback drinking *pastis* at the bar. There are no underage girls, there is no procurer, and there is no sex. But we're dealing here with Sandrine's versions of reality. Whether or not men went upstairs with women at the *Miel du Midi*, or they sat around drinking *pastis* is not important: what matters is that Sandrine had decided her husband was cheating on her. She named the girls and complained he reeked of their perfumes when he came home. Nothing he said would dissuade her. Her interest in cosmology came in here. There was not one but many universes, she maintained, and in one of them Nimmo was screwing the girls upstairs in the *Miel du Midi.*

We had to get to know Sandrine after the event. We knew that she liked particle physics, that she 'had', as the French say, fifty-five years. Add to that she had auburn hair, no children and she saw visions.

She also had an ability to tell countries by the noises they made, in the dark especially. Everyone who knew her vouches for it. She could perceive countries, actual land masses, as sound pictures or audio maps. Islands, archipelagos, republics, emirates – all made sounds she could hear and identify. She 'heard' them in much the way Rimbaud 'saw' the colours of vowels. In her ear each had a call-sign. Like radio stations.

When friends dropped by they invariably asked Sandrine, 'So how is Greece sounding today?' And Sandrine would listen to the Grecian internal signal and say, 'Greece is all sirens this morning.'

And if you asked her about some smaller, lesser-known place, Sandrine was always equal to the task. 'Réunion… ? Last night, Réunion was the sound of candles, hot wax and sputtering wicks.'

If Sandrine listened to countries and continents the way some people listen to music, she also took physics very personally. She was outspoken about modern science in a frank, intimate way and so, of course, when friends tried to explain it, they would say, 'Well, the husband's twenty years older than she is.'

Sandrine read popular physics magazines the way Madame Bovary read cheap novelettes. She marked her favourite passages on reality machines and quantum computers, and Nimmo told Siggie that there was something very alarming about seeing these books filled with charts and diagrams, maths and magic.

'I know for a fact she was no good at arithmetic at school.'

Sandrine was very taken with the idea behind the quantum computer; she'd bring it up in the middle of any conversation. She knew that recently scientists had succeeded in transferring information between molecules, a small start but the quantum computer was on its way.

When the postman came by one morning, Sandrine grabbed him and told him – straight to his face, 'The trouble with current computers is this: *reality*. Too many factors to compute. Too slow. Maybe one day we can programme movement and sexual desire into a computer. Someday soon. Sure. But how do you run through all the shades of meaning attached to love or death? How do you make it laugh or cry? Too many numbers. Only a quantum computer can do that. We'll be able to perform very complex sums very much faster when we can crack bigger numbers. If you rev the internal life of the computer up to bigger speeds, you solve more problems. Or, put it this way, you manufacture more reality. We'll be able to programme our own universes.'

She went on to tell the postman about the theory that there existed not one but many universes, packed together like bubbles on a head of beer. The multiverse explained a mystery in quantum physics: why a thing might be and not be – Hamlet's quandary compounded – at the same time. Why particles could be in two places at once, and why the same cat, gassed to death in one cat box, might be discovered hale and hearty in another.

She must have enjoyed cell biology, too, because among the piles of science magazines she kept, Nimmo found she had marked a passage in *Popular Genetics*: 'Soon a cell from the tip of your nose will be sufficient to grow another you!' Beside it, in angry black eyebrow pencil, she had scrawled, 'Not if I have anything to do with it.'

That was shortly before it happened.

On one of those Friday nights when her husband was at the *Miel du Midi*, at around 10.30 Sandrine left the neat bedroom on the second floor of the big house above Mazamet and came downstairs in her nightdress, and the toes of her Turkish slippers poked out enquiringly from beneath the hem of her blue dressing-gown. She carried a can of petrol – Elf, as it happens – bought that afternoon from the service station on the corner of the street and sealed with a plastic cap. She had in one pocket of her midnight-blue gown a box of long matches, which her husband used to light his Havana cigars.

In her other pocket she carried a pistol, and not just any pistol – that would've been to miss the point and she was not intending to miss anything – but the .38 that Nimmo had bought, quite illegally, from Jules, the policeman. Officers were not permitted to flog their weapons – or civilians to buy them, but if you have a lot of treasure in your house then you need some form of protection and her husband had aeroplanes and vintage cars; any number of grandfather clocks, some very rare with silver faces, with many keys, with softly chiming hours like liquid heartbeats; and Spanish carvings of the grieving virgin and her crucified son, and lots of big black, oaken cupboards. She had loaded the pistol earlier, taking the rounds from the white linen bag beneath the bed where her husband thought he had hidden them.

The hills and valleys of the Tarn were sunk in the most profound torpor that spring night, and even the frogs slept. France, as Sandrine listened, did not make its usual sound, a small mewing, like a hungry cat swallowing milk.

At 11 precisely she picked up her petrol canister and began dousing the outside walls of the barn; she did the same to the house. At 11.10, knowing that her husband was exactly five minutes away, she lit a long match and threw it into the petrol. The fire blazed and in no time at all you could see the faces of the lions on the gateposts. She took the pistol from the other pocket. It was cold in the garden and yet the gun slipped in her hand. She was sweating.

At 11.15 she turned to face the lions on the gateposts at the end of the driveway and sighted down the barrel. It was just for show – she was not ready yet. The heat from the barn and house was now quite pleasant and the popping sounds of the flames reminded her, vaguely, of Romania. This was the plan. Her husband would stop the car, so appalled by the blazing house, and the barn, which was even now beginning to fall inwards, in great fiery ropes of silver and gold, that he would stand there in terror as his treasures perished in front of his terrified eyes. At this moment she would shoot him.

Why did she do it? There is no answer to this question, not the questions of cloning, not the belief that the nightclub might have been a brothel, not the noises in her head. Local people shrug and say that Sandrine 'lost her mind'. But that won't do either. That is the worst of answers. Sandrine's mind was good enough to enjoy the particularities of modern physics and the possibilities of great genetic advances. It brought her, in her Turkish slippers, by way of majestic stage management, to standing, gun in hand, outside the burning house.

Siggie liked to point out that there was a chance that Nimmo, after she shot him in this world, might still be alive and kicking in the universe next door. Indeed, if there are an infinite number of universes then it was certain he'd be there, right down to his tiny hands and his vintage cars. But, happily, for her, for us, we can never know what happens in the universe next door.

'And Sandrine would have been content knowing that at least he was as dead as a doornail in this one'.

Now the flames were roaring, the lower floors of the house were blazing, the clocks caught fire and died in a muffled clang of their movements, like wounded men. The flames worked their way into the rafters of the barn and began raising the roof. Sandrine could see them dancing in the windows, and through the panes she watched Nimmo's vintage cars glow and pulse and seem to throb in the heat. Their paint blistered and peeled in flakes of red and blue.

And still her husband did not come.

A few minutes later the windows began shattering, a column of smoke stood up like a fist over the houses and the barn and in the distance Sandrine could hear what she first thought must be Bulgaria, a long, low singing the night. But when it got louder it turned into a siren and the siren turned into a fire engine – and still Nimmo did not sweep up the drive between the sleeping marble lions, their faces rosy as if they had a fever, seeming to be growling and gnawing at their paws as the temperature soared. Nimmo's arrival time sometimes varied by anything up to ten minutes. She knew that, she had allowed for that, but not for the speed and the fury of the inferno. The fire was so loud and the roof beams were cracking and still her husband was not there. The Tiger Moth and the Messerschmitt caught fire now, their tails glistening like peacocks' tails. The firemen aimed jets of water into the inferno. And still he had not come.

Sandrine had so little time to act. She had such a desire for things to be final, and she was appalled at her husband's inconstancy, his unreliability. Never before had he failed to return promptly – he was a punctual man. She could not have known he was delayed by the very engines that raced to his house.

The roof fell in now, the firemen came closer. They didn't see the woman at the end of the drive. Their hoses sent ropes of white water twisting into the hot, angry heart of the fire.

Slowly Sandrine raised the little .38. Just then the flames reached inside the Porsches in their stable and their fuel tanks began exploding. The sound of the shot was as nothing in the night.

It is not possible to know why she did it. But what she did had an awful symmetry. It says something about her mind. She liked things to be… elegant. To be shapely, to add up, to be conclusive; and when Nimmo failed to arrive, she weighted the scales the other way.

And that's when Nimmo arrived, riding ahead of several more

94

fire engines, to see his house spitting flame, to hear the fuel tanks of his vintage cars exploding, and to see his wife lying in the driveway, with the pistol in her hand.

The house was a write-off and the goods inside carried no insurance. The grandfather clocks were a ruined forest but a few had escaped with burns and some water damage. Siggie bought four and sanded the wounds of the fire from their lovely brown cases. The cupboards, the old commodes, the coats of arms, which Nimmo had kept in the house, were badly scorched and cracked. Jules the gendarme bought them at fire-sale prices and sold them on at the market in La Grande Ronde in Toulouse, pulling as much as three times his asking price for a smoky eighteenth-century peachwood armoire.

Of the three Porsches Nimmo had kept like stuffed poodles in the barn, two were salvaged, resprayed, retooled and returned to their pedestals. Nimmo never repaired the house; instead, he backed a caravan into the fire-shrivelled interior and lived there. The front of the caravan was his office and the rear was his bedroom. The salvaged Porsches rested on either side of the caravan like watchdogs. Out in the driveway the lions lay on their plinths, gnawing their forepaws.

Siggie dreams of buying those lions. He's had photographs taken and carries them around in his wallet and shows them to anyone who has the slightest interest in doing a deal. But he needs a partner and he needs a truck.

'They're the purest white marble and you would need a crane to lift them,' he says happily. 'They must be worth thousands.'

I think of this often.

St Francis in the Veld

The De Tromp family, Tookie and his wife Tina, lived on the farm Lamentation, out in the Red Hills, with their son, little Jamie, who got religious later.

Some said Jamie got religious because his dad was righteous. Others said, yes, no, OK, but Tookie got righteous in the wrong way. Not purely righteous, like the British Israelites, who lived out Nickleton way, and said they were descended in an unbroken line from Eve to the Royal Family of England.

Tookie got righteous after he was told by the ministry of agriculture that he had to improve the facilities for the wandering folk, shearers and fence menders, who rode their donkey carts from farm to farm, pots and pans tied to the cart with baling wire, not a cent in their pockets or food in the bellies of their scraggy kids. Looking for a farmer with a few sheep, or a bad fence where the jackals took the sheep. They had nothing, these folk, and when they made a bit they blew it on sweet white wine and dancing and the getting of yet more skinny kids. Never had a roof, a bed, a table – just pulled the rusty sheets of corrugated iron from beneath the cart, lit a fire and made camp for the night. 'Swervers' they were called – or 'wanderers'.

Nobody liked them – not farmers, labourers or town dwellers. Too rough and ready, and too damn reckless. It made people want to spit just to see their tracks on the dusty road, two long scribbles where the rubber tyres rolled this way and that through the hot silence of the empty land. You could have built them palaces, and they'd maybe stay for a while – then one day, out of the blue, the call would come…

'My blood is up,' they'd say.

Next morning they had struck camp and were gone.

For these people Tookie had been told he must build outhouses. Flush toilets. Running water. Septic tanks. Monthly collection by the Lutherburg Sanitary Services.

'Righteous anger was just welling up in me,' Tookie told Donnie over a beer at the Hunter's Arms.

'Welling?' Donnie frowned.

Tookie nodded. 'Up and up. Like a borehole.'

'Hell man, Tookie! Listen, brother, like a volcano, hey? You know why's that?'

'No, I don't know why's that,' Tookie said. Even though he did.

'It's because the Last Days is coming. There is signs.'

Donnie always said that. Donnie was a British Israelite and the Last Days were his big thing. He'd once been just another farmer over towards Scorpionpoint, big bare legs, tiny denim shorts, thick cotton socks and nothing much in his head but rugby and docking sheep's tails, drought and shooting springbok. Normal stuff. Then one day he got the call, sold up and moved over Nickleton way, where the Israelites had their temple. Living in a little shack he hung a poster on the back of his bedroom door. It was the family tree of the true lost tribe of the British Israelites, ruby branches glowing like a candelabra. All the others were fakes. The sacred line of the true Israelites of Nickleton ran from Adam and Eve, in Eden, to Queen Elizabeth in England, straight to Donnie in Nickleton.

For Donnie everything came down to the signs, especially the volcanoes disgorging lava that would crisp the planet. There had never been volcanic activity near Nickleton but that didn't mean it wasn't on its way. In the Last Days everyone was for the high jump. Everyone except the British Israelites because their God Yahweh was backing them.

Donnie was forever seeing the signs.

'Say you're driving to Beaufort West. You see a woman hitching – OK? Do not give her a lift.' He dropped his voice so that the barman, Mike the Spike, serving doubles in the corner, wouldn't hear him. 'It's a plot, OK?'

'What's a plot?'

'Certain women getting you to sleep with them. Then they take your sperm prisoner.'

'Why'd they do that?'

'They need your brain power. How else do they get it? That's the plot – OK? They're planning to grab our genetic codes. Yahweh's warned us. OK?'

Donnie was always trying to sell the Israelite angle. The world was almost overs-cadovers. Join now and be saved.

But Tookie wasn't buying. He bought only what he saw and touched, and he had seen and touched the government letter instructing him to erect suitable water-closets and septic tanks for his itinerant shearers. Tookie didn't like it, his righteous anger was welling up all the time, but it was in writing and so he did it.

His wife Tina did not like it either.

She was a little pale, faintly blonde woman with good ankles and broad shoulders, and she sat on the sofa beneath the giant gold wristwatch that hung on the wall beside the views of the Snow Mountains, talking to Bella-Louise, the doll in her lap, a very clever person with big green eyes and skin smooth as butter.

Tookie's building work happened a long way from the farmhouse. But Bella-Louise told Tina that if they used the sights on Tookie's hunting rifle that would give them a good view. Tina had a peep and, as usual, Bella-Louise was right. Through the telescopic sights Tina watched the towers of grey breezeblocks growing on a patch of veld.

'Dear Heaven, no good will come of this.'

Tina told Tookie and he said, 'How did you see what I was doing?' And she showed him. 'Hell, that's not a bad idea,' he said.

Next thing, they learnt that Tookie had arranged for the jam wagon to trundle out to Lamentation once a week and pump the stuff out of the septic tanks, just like it did in Lutherburg.

Tina looked down at Bella-Louise. 'Did we marry this man to be touched by the clatter of the town? Or did we come here for the peace and privacy of the far country where people do not visit and each day is peaceful under heaven?'

Bella-Louise opened her green eyes wide as windows and replied, 'Peace and privacy.'

Tina asked Bella-Louise if she wished for the town to come to the farm and Bella-Louise shook her head. She asked Bella-Louise if she wanted the horrid building to stop and for the breezeblocks to come tumbling down – and Bella-Louise clapped her hands. Tina asked Bella-Louise if she could love someone who fell to building little houses in the veld, and Bella-Louise shook her head and pressed her knees together. Tina asked Bella-Louise what would happen to her poor son, Jamie, when the town came to the farm, and Bella-Louise trembled.

And yet, at least to begin with, Jamie seemed fine. A pale fellow, very quiet and older than his years. He had always been a keen farmer. Driving the tractor when he was just seven, managing the Toyota bakkie by ten, a fine shot in the springbok season.

But as Jamie saw the outhouses going up and listened to his mother talking to her doll, he worked even harder. And he got quieter. Every morning after breakfast he slipped on his earphones and was off to the fields, with his radio tuned to Radio Salvation – 'Your station for non-stop prayer and rejoicing in the Lord.' It wasn't any particular choice, he tuned in because reception was bad around Lamentation, and Radio Salvation had the best signal.

As Tookie's righteous anger welled up in him, he spent more and more time on his project, so the day-to-day farm work fell to Jamie. He was in charge of dipping the sheep; he began patching the mud wall of the dam against the next year's rains – if these ever came; he got the fences fixed.

Around December-time a travelling family of swervers turned up in their donkey carts. For Tookie this was D-Day. His righteous anger had brought forth the desired result. Three outhouses stood ready. Modern, the best you could build, ceramic cisterns, good chains, real wooden handles and a sheaf of pages torn from the *Farmer's Weekly* strung though a hoop of baling wire on the back of each neat green door.

Tookie directed the new arrivals into the field he'd prepared; he was as excited as a man reversing a new harvester into his barn. Here was the test!

The swervers outspanned their donkeys and tuned their radio to the faint crackle of a far-away rock station. That was the thing about the travellers – they had no work or no money, but the radio was always playing music, loud and crass. Tom was a thin man with high cheekbones and narrow eyes and his wife Klara wore an old red headscarf and she looked very young to have three kids. Their names, Tom told Tookie, were Sticky Thing, Little Nothing and Hippo Girl. The children held tight to their mother's legs, and then ran off to play with a rusty old bicycle wheel and a crude catapult.

Tookie had no shearing for the swervers but he set them to lining his fences with rocks to stop jackals tunnelling under the wire and taking his sheep. Tom and Klara toiled in the white heat of the summer sun, heaving boulders on to a hand cart and pushing it along the wire fence that ran straight as a knife across the freckled koppies.

The swervers camped by their cart at night in the place where he had built the outhouses and he saw the glow of their fire of an evening. Each morning he checked out the distant camp through the telescopic sights of his hunting rifle. All seemed as it should be. Until one day he drove over to take a closer look at how they were getting on.

He drove straight back to the farm and told his wife, 'They are using the paper to light the fire, all the paper that hung on the doors.'

Bella-Louise looked up at him with her green eyes. 'Well, what do you expect if you play with fire?'

But Tookie was used to misunderstanding what the doll said.

'Getting to grips takes time. Give them a chance.'

And he cut more pages from *Farmer's Weekly* and hung it behind the doors of the outhouses. And he spent a lot of time pointing his rifle at the horizon and wondering what to do if they misused the paper again.

When the school year ended Tina and Bella-Louise talked a lot about letting Jamie go to the new Christian school in Lutherburg because the village school was filled with township kids. It wasn't about anything but keeping up standards, and belief in the Lord, said Tina.

'It's about the boy's future, and him being a Christian.' Bella-Louise gave a firm shake of her pretty porcelain head.

Jamie didn't have much say in it but, then, he was an amenable boy. He worked all day in the fields, singing hymns from the radio.

'The Lord is My Country/My Future and my Past/I shall live in Him/From First to Last.'

Tookie drove out to the camp and he found they'd done it again. Then he went into Lutherburg and bawled out the Town Clerk because the order to build outhouses had come from the town municipality. But the clerk said he was sorry – he just passed on the ministry of agriculture's instructions about sanitary arrangements for farm workers. It was none of his business what people did with the sanitary arrangements built for them.

Tookie went over the Hunter's Arms and had a beer with Pascal Le Gros who told him not to worry. 'It is simple, my friend. Just don't replace the paper, OK? People got rights. But they also got responsibilities. They got to learns – use it or lose it, that's democratic…'

But Tookie couldn't do that. It wasn't about politics – it was about doing things properly. And he tried even harder. The righteousness was so strong in him that he just went on cutting up old copies of *Farmer's Weekly*, really fast. Then he settled down with his rifle to watch them through the telescopic sights. And just as fast he saw the paper burn.

But he did not let up. He gave Tom and Klara a goat for slaughtering at Christmas. And a five-litre bag of sweet white wine. For their children there was a catapult, a small plastic machine gun and a rubber ball. To his family it seemed the worse his footloose workers behaved, the more Tookie gave them.

'He's mad!' said Tina to Bella-Louise, and Bella-Louise nodded.

On Christmas Day Tookie, Tina, Bella-Louise and Jamie sat down to roast lamb, but it was an uncomfortable lunch. Jamie said grace and it went on for about five minutes because of all the people he prayed to God to save. Besides sinners and adulterers and captains of industry, he prayed also for those who took from the Lord the righteousness that was His alone and spent it on the base things of this world.

'Right,' said Tina. 'Very base.'

'You can't find baser things anywhere,' said Bella-Louise.

But Tookie wasn't listening. He was wolfing down his food, keen to get back to his seat by the window and his telescopic sights. He sat there for maybe five minutes. Tookie watched the nomads circling the remains of their fire and he could see the headless carcass of the goat he'd given them for roasting. Tom and Karla were carrying enamel mugs which he was sure contained the white wine he had also given them. Of their children, there was no sign. Sent off to mind the donkeys while Tom and Klara were busy making more children, bold as brass, on Christmas Day.

'Come here and take a look-see at this, hey!'

'No, thank you,' said Tina. 'I've got better things to do on Christmas Day than to stare at some old Hottentots.'

But Bella-Louise said she would have a quick peep. Tina helped her to put her green eye to the rifle sights and Bella-Louise squealed. Tom and Klara moved around the fire, hand in hand, in a kind of rutting dance. Tookie knew that their radio beside them on the ground was churning out rock 'n' roll. Tom was naked from the waist up and Klara wore nothing at all.

Then Jamie had a look and when he did he grew very pale and turned on Radio Salvation so loud Bella-Louise covered her ears, and the boy left the house, saying he was off to dock sheep's tails.

Tookie offered the women another look but Bella-Louise buried her head in Tina's bosom. 'There now,' said Tina. 'You've upset her. I hope you're satisfied, Mr Righteous Anger!'

The next morning when Tookie lifted his rifle to his eye he saw nothing.

He drove over to the camp. He found the fire still smouldering, the goat's head lying where they had sawn it off, the eyes bruised and pleading. He knew the story. Tom and Klara had heard the call – their blood was up and they had vanished. His feeling of righteous anger was welling up more strongly than ever as he began stamping out the remains of their fire. That was when he noticed that pools of water had formed around the outhouses.

Pushing open a door, he found something so awful he had to retreat to his Toyota and sit there for a few minutes before he recovered sufficiently to go and take a closer look, his handkerchief pressed to his nose.

His eyes had not fooled him. Since they had burnt all the paper, they had resorted to using small round stones and then dropped them into the bowl. When one lavatory had flooded they had moved to the next. What did he expect? They were nomads, they moved on.

Some people see the light on the road, others hear divine commandments. Tookie's moment of revelation came in a glimpse of a pile of stones sunk in murky water. A revelation so strong he could not but obey it. Otherwise, surely he would have called his workers to clean out the mess. But he did not do so.

When the story began to spread, the farmers around the area were worried, guilty, angry. 'I don't believe it,' they said. 'The guy must be crazy, OK?'

For Tookie removed the stones himself, he cleared the blockage, restrung the sheaves of paper and hung them on the back of each door. And, before long, another travelling family was camped in the field. And each time the same thing repeated itself – paper into the fire, stones into the bowls – and each time Tookie cleaned it out, not because he liked it, or them, but because his righteous anger welled up like lava. He tightened his lips and he said to himself, 'Right, then, just you see who gives in first!'

He began building more outhouses. Nor did he stop being righteous even when young Jamie said he wanted to be a weekly boarder in the new Christian school in Lutherburg because the government school was the 'territory of Lucifer', being full of kids who, said Jamie, 'loved lechery'.

Tina and Bella-Louise got Jamie's trunk ready for the new school and they sewed his costume for Remembrance Day when the boys in waistcoats and the girls in tutus of blue, white and orange danced around the flagpole from which flew the old national flag, as they sang the former national anthem.

On the first day of term, Donnie came to talk to the Christian school and warned the kids about genetic codes and the end of the world, though the headmaster asked particularly that there be no mention of sperm, so Donnie told them instead about the Antichrist.

'He lives in New York with a lot of Jews and Masons and plans to steal your genetic code by methods which you will learn about when you are older.'

Young Jamie lapped it up, he got more and more religious and he began to talk like Radio Salvation, mixed in with the British Israelite stuff he got from Donnie.

It is pretty unsettling, people said, when a twelve-year-old boy tells perfect strangers, 'My ambition is to labour in the Lord's vineyards all the days of my youth. I pray for my people and my culture. My favourite sport is rugby and when I am older my favourite occupation will be fighting the Antichrist.'

At weekends he went home to Lamentation where he was more useful than ever, mending fences and checking the dam walls because his father was toiling among six new outhouses. Tookie swore that if six did not break his spirit, why, then, let him build another six, nine, twelve, and see what the wanderers would do with those. He wasn't giving up or going under. Let them destroy – he would clean and restore and build anew.

This stuff sent the people in Lutherburg dippy when they wandered in for a beer and let fly at Pascal le Gros at the Hunter's Arms.

'What a bloody family! Look at the wife – talking to dolls, and the son trying to be a *dominee* before he's fifteen, and the old man building a suburb of lavatories. A slave to his servants. Up to his elbows in… He has embarrassed the hell out of everyone…'

It brought strangers, foreigners, into town, all wanting to see this mad guy. They asked about him at the Hunter's Arms. And Pascal le Gros told his barman Mike the Spike he had an idea.

'Pilgrims, that's what they are. I swear to God. People overseas, they go to Lourdes for miracles. OK? Hey? Well, why always go for foreign saints? Answer me that. We got our own holy Joe right there. He is making up for all the past, he is reaching out, he is doing penance. Let's support him, hey?'

But there were some people who did not like this. They told him, 'Shame, leave the guy alone, Pascal. Can't you see he's cuckoo?'

Pascal's face purpled up to something past aubergine and he hooked his hands under his belly and shifted it the way a man rocks a heavy boulder. 'Why hide his light under a bushel, my friends? Bugger that! This is a new country now. We got to reach out to each other. And we need the trade. People are coming to Lutherburg to see the spring flowers – don't they? And the petri-fied dinosaur footprints. So why not come to see a local miracle?'

'No bloody ways,' said the guys in the bar. 'If this is a miracle, you can keep it.'

'You guys wouldn't know a miracle if it bit you in the bum,' said Pascal le Gros. 'I'll find people who do have eyes to see. Who do have a bit of class. Who are open to the wonders of the life of the spirit. City people, foreigners, classy pilgrims.'

It was a good deal, Pascal's weekend package at the Hunter's Arms. Half-board and guaranteed sightings of the miracle worker on organised visits to 'the shrine'. The pilgrims arrived by coach on Fridays. When they got off the coach from Cape Town, they were greeted by Mike the Spike with a complimentary cocktail.

'Holy water, anyone? White wine, slug of gin, crème de menthe, maraschino cherry.'

Friday night was karaoke night in the ladies' bar. On Saturday there was a visit to the observatory at Sutherland followed by Karoo cuisine at its finest, a lamb *braai*. Sunday was the pilgrimage proper, the Faith in the Veld Excursion.

Before leaving the hotel Pascal gave the pilgrims a briefing. 'Just think you're going to the Vatican. Or a mosque. Or Jerusalem. Some similar sacred place. So, *respect* – right? Gentlemen, no bare feet, please. Ladies, no shorts. What you will see is the miracle of Lutherburg, a man born to be master waiting humbly on his servants in the veld. A proud man serving the poorest of the poor. Our St Francis.'

And when Donnie the British Israelite said, 'St Francis didn't do outhouses, he was mad about animals,' Pascal said, 'So what is the bloody diffs, hey? It is not the outhouse *qua* outhouse that we are looking at here – it is the spiritual import.'

At eleven sharp, Mike the Spike, in his cherry-red pick-up, led the coach of pilgrims over the dusty roads to Lamentation and parked upwind of the farm. After a picnic lunch and a couple of glasses of wine the pilgrims were led on foot through the veld to within viewing range, a raised outcrop of rock where Pascal had built a hide from reeds and mud.

Through binoculars, the visitors would study Tookie slaving amongst the outhouses, bucket in hand. In this field, in this forest, in this cathedral of small grey towers, to and fro like a soldier, an army, selfless, unstoppable, marched the saint.

'No photographs, please,' Mike the Spike reminded the pilgrims. Afterwards he took tips.

The Violin

I once knew a man who thought he was a singing dog.

Fred was the janitor, odd-job man, resident wraith of an apartment building halfway up the rue de Seine, where I lived in the seventies.

The rue de Seine then was a quiet place, bookish, listless, slightly scuffed. There was the river, the Beaux-Arts and the muffled blare of the boulevards at the end of the street. The little hotel where Oscar Wilde died, deploring the wallpaper, was up the street towards the river. The café on the corner filled slowly with odd and disconsolate types who always looked as if they were rehearsing more colourful roles. The calmness of the street was misleading. The quarter had begun to catch the eye of those urban predators, the developers. Our block was marked for improvement. Several tenants in the older, shabbier apartments had been given notice to quit. We were fighting the changes but we knew it was only a question of time.

In our old building there lived, besides the concierge, a couple of profs from the Ecôle Normale, a retired fencing master in a blue skull cap who was as sleek and as shapely as a banister, an architect, an optometrist and Madame Pujols, the florist, who was secretary of the Central Committee of the local Communist Party. Raymond Duncan had once lived in the building and he'd built a theatre inside the house. No one had danced there for decades but sometimes someone arranged a concert. The old fencing master particularly liked piano trios, Madame Pujols had been a singer before she became a florist, and I had a weakness for solo violin. Old, fading photos of Isadora Duncan dancing in gauzy veils, and of Raymond, wearing a snowy caftan and sandals, portly amid a throng of his mistresses all wearing the same homespun robes, looking like chubby Druids, were tacked to the theatre walls.

The last of Raymond Duncan's devotees still lived in the building. White haired, and white robed, she clacked in her clogs across the cobbles of the courtyard in the morning to clean the little theatre.

Fred came to France from Morocco before the war, still a boy. The invasion of France had frozen Fred in time. He believed Paris was still occupied by German troops, and though those days were long past, he still never left the building without an elaborate check to see whether he was being spied on. Once out in the street he kept doubling back on himself in case he was being followed.

Fred slept in a skinny brass bed in the tiny attic, in the eaves of the seventeenth-century roof. It was not a bedroom, it was hiding place, and he kept under his brass bed a bag ready packed, just in case the Germans came looking for him. For thirty years he hid out under the arching struts that reminded me of the ribcage of a whale.

Fred looked after us and we tried to do the same for him, though it was not easy. He minded the boilers, swept the courtyard and the corridors, and sometimes he cleaned a few windows. He sang Moroccan songs. We kept him like a house pet. But, then, what were we to do with him? His terror of being denounced was so real – and we collaborated in his fear. When he was functioning, he could just about look after himself. When he forgot to change his clothes, Madame Pujols found him new ones; when he omitted to wash, I stood him in the bath and hosed him down. He lived on donations of vegetables, bread and salami, which we left outside his door.

His anxieties were not necessary but there was no telling that to Fred. Many years earlier Madame Pujols had fixed his papers; she even had applied for and received a passport.

One day, some time in 1977, Madame Pujols decided to visit Moscow in much the way invalids in the hope of a cure make a pilgrimage to Lourdes. She thought that a trip to the shrine where Lenin saw the light might clear Fred's foggy mind. And he went along – willingly or not, I could not say. You never could tell with Fred. But knowing his old fears and thinking to reassure him, Madame Pujols had told him that in the last war the USSR had been a great opponent of Nazi Germany. Naturally, she did not tell him that it had also been for a time a willing ally. But, then, Fred had no notion of what an ally was. And I suppose it never occurred to him that the Soviet Union was anything more than an extension of the rue de Seine. Chances are he wouldn't have known where one ended and the other began since,

Madame Pujols told us later, he kept his eyes closed throughout the flight.

When he opened them again, they were in Moscow, lodged in enormous bedrooms on separate floors at the Hotel Ukraina. It was only when Madame Pujols set off to visit her comrades that Fred stuck his nose out, sniffed the air and went on a little field trip of his own.

The Ukraina, with its huge bedrooms, its unexpected ballrooms, its stretches of tatty red carpet, its hundreds of chandeliers, dangling like electric mushrooms from its crumbling ceilings, was a fine place for Fred. It was closed, stuffy, practically empty, it was indoors. In short, it was safe – and he never set foot outside. This suited Madame Pujols and Fred. Each evening he would tell her about the adventures of the day and, sensible traveller as she was, she confessed that he had seen and done much more than she had ever managed to do in Moscow.

'It was the beginning of him, and his repertoire. I went to Party meetings. But Fred went to concerts.'

And in a way Madame Pujols's wish to change his life when she took him to Moscow really came about – even if he didn't derive inner strength from proximity to the people's paradise, a Muscovite miracle of sorts did occur. Madame Pujols would often at this point in her story hum a few bars of that old Stalinist patriotic children's song: 'We were born to make fairy-tales a reality…'

Fred's fairy had been a floor lady.

He noticed her on his first morning. She sat at the far end of the immensely long corridor. Each floor had one. She watched, noted and, from time to time, reported on the comings and goings of the guests. It was perfectly normal. Fred's floor lady was a very pretty young woman, very much like a Russian doll, with porcelain skin, honeyed hair and china-blue eyes. Her only flaw, really, was a purple and brown bruise about the size of a golf ball on her milky neck.

Her name was Yuliah, and she spoke a few words of French, picked up over the years from foreign visitors whom she longingly studied for their air of assurance, their freedom to come and go.

'Where do you come from?' Yuliah asked Fred in her heavily inflected French.

Fred thought it was a game. He was fascinated by the way she spoke, and delightedly he mimicked her.

'Whaaar you come frrrommm... ?'

She shook her head, laughing at his exact echo of her words, and pointed at him. 'Not me – you!'

'I come from here,' said Fred.

'And where is here?'

Fred didn't know. He came close to her and with a trembling hand he touched the dark stain on her neck.

'Does it hurt?'

Yuliah smiled. 'It's nothing. It comes from the playing.'

The next morning when Yuliah returned to her desk it had been polished, the defunct candelabra overhead had been dusted and the plastic pen that did not work had been placed on the leather blotter for which, from somewhere, Fred had salvaged a piece of blue blotting paper. And in a small tooth glass taken from his room there stood a single plastic tulip, taken from the large bunch of plastic tulips that stood like some bad Dutch joke in the dusty ballroom.

She was very moved and, to thank him, the next day she

114

brought with her a violin, which she fitted to the scar on her neck. She played him Russian folk songs, each of which she announced. First came *'Ochie Chernye'* – Black Eyes – a tune perfect for the shameless sentiment of the fiddle. Fred wept, and fat tears splashed on to the desk and were soaked up by blue blotting paper. Then came 'Moscow Nights' and then 'Coachman, Don't Speed the Horses', then 'Wild Strawberries', then a gypsy 'Czardas', a Cossack dance, and at the end a folk song from Siberia, because she came from there.

It was a concert, but it was also a conversion.

On the day they were due to leave Moscow, Fred caused Madame Pujols several moments of anxiety when he locked himself in his bedroom and refused to come out. It was Yuliah who solved the problem – she knocked softly on the door and told him that she would come to him in Paris.

'With the violin?' asked Fred.

'With the violin.'

'All right,' said Fred.

Fred began preparing as soon as he got home, sweeping his hiding place under the rafters, placing a single flower, a rose, a tulip, an iris, which Madame Pujols gave him each day, in a Perrier bottle beside his brass bed, and saying to everyone, 'She is coming, you know.'

It was very literal, his insistence. She was coming to him.

It wasn't easy to get a visa for a visiting student, which was the way we framed our application. But we had the persuasive letter from Madame Pujols to her colleagues in Moscow, and we had the support of the profs from the Sorbonne, who were good communists all. We cited the proximity of the Sorbonne; we talked vaguely of Yuliah furthering her studies at the École des Beaux-Arts. And it worked. We got her a six-month visa, with the assurance that she would live with Madame Pujols, who would defray her expenses.

It was hard to explain to Fred that Yuliah would not be living in his room. He kept saying, 'Why not?' And polishing the brass bed, and rearranging the flower, and clasping his hands together. The best we could do was to repeat that Yuliah was coming for sure.

'With the violin?'

'With the violin,' said the old fencing master.

Yuliah arrived one evening and we all went to meet her in Madame Pujols's apartment. We had showered Fred and dressed him in good dungarees and blue shirt, and cut and combed his hair. Yuliah shone, pale and exquisite, like a stalactite. She put out her hand to Fred, and when he did not take it, she leaned forward and kissed him on the cheek. Fred stood like a sentry, his eyes down and his toes pressed together. The room was full of people wanting to meet her. Madame Pujols offered aperitifs, people lit cigarettes, they chatted – about Moscow, Brezhnev and the Party.

Stepping close to Yuliah, Fred very gently touched the mark on her neck. His eyes were on the violin. But Madame Pujols said, 'She can't play tonight. Look at the girl, Fred – she's exhausted.'

'Tomorrow I will play for Fred,' said Yuliah.

The next night, in Madame Pujols's sitting room, with Fred at her feet, she played for us. Alone. Listening to solo violin is an acquired taste. Playing is something that takes great skill because the least flaw shows. I suppose, after Fred's adoration and the stories of Madame Pujols when she got back from Moscow, I'd somehow expected a virtuoso. Yuliah was a pretty player – no more. Thin vibrato, shaky on the upper registers. And, of course, there was no reason why she should have been better. The fiddle was simply something she did. It was not a vision of heaven.

But she looked so good. She like to lift her chin high before settling the instrument, to lift even higher her bow as she began a new piece, as if cracking a whip in slow motion. Her repertoire ran from dances and laments to love songs, from heart-rending schmaltz to high-wire dazzle.

It was Fred who made up for anything she lacked musically – he was a virtuoso audience. He never moved. He ate her up.

For a while after that she played whenever Fred bounded up with her fiddle in his paw. But there were many new things for her. She worked on her French. She enrolled in the Beaux-Arts. Fred would trail her to the gates in the rue Bonaparte, and her friends would laugh and say, not unkindly, about her small dark adorer, 'Who's your faithful follower?' Yuliah would say, 'Oh, that's just Fred…' and wave her pale fingers as she was swept away.

He did seem doglike in his love. But, then, he had always been a kind of pet to us too.

And he must have felt it because one day he said to Yuliah, 'I am the singing dog.'

She shook her head, appalled. 'No, Fred – anyway, dogs don't sing.'

She began avoiding him after that, she got colder. The weather inside the house got noticeably worse.

She tried hiding the fiddle.

Fred thought that was a terrific game. He sniffed it out once again and raced up to her, practically wagging his tail.

And Yuliah began to say no.

Fred didn't listen. In fact, he couldn't listen, he was what he was and so was she. For all her delicacy, Yuliah possessed a kind of polar core. Fred had fallen in love with the Siberian winter. He was lost in the permafrost – and he wasn't dressed for it.

One day, Fred asked her up to his room – to talk, not to play, he promised. But when she was inside the hiding place, he locked the door and fetched the fiddle from under his bed, and sat there, panting.

Yuliah took the fiddle, lifted it to her chin and then in a single easy movement tossed it out of the window to land three stories down in the rue de Seine, where a passing Peugeot crushed it flat before Fred could unlock his door and race down the stairs.

He came back up the stairs holding the violin by its broken neck, passing Yuliah on her way down, and tried to give it back to her, but she turned him away with a flick of her fingers.

He made several attempts to fix the instrument. He used Scotch tape, he even strapped it in bandages. Then one day I found it in the trash can. And we thought he was over it.

In fact, it was beginning. He'd be in the courtyard watering the flowers, or he'd be standing at the far end of the corridor staring at the wall, when he'd slowly raise a violin to his shoulder. He'd tune it then, lifting his bowing arm in a gesture very much like Yuliah's but surer and smoother, he'd begin.

Of course, there was nothing there. There was only Fred, in the silence.

He was very good. He moved easily between positions, his bowing arm was lovely, he had the bravura; he had the slow sob and the hi-jinks: he had just about everything it takes a finished fiddler to string us along. He had it all – except the violin.

And so what? What is playing the fiddle? Scraping a shank of horsehair over slivers of sheep-gut pegged to a wooden box. I'd say he was as good as the real thing; and it's not all that often the real thing is as good as Fred.

He even had a mark on his neck from all his practising, just like Yuliah. He was very proud of his scar.

He didn't take bookings. Fred was impromptu. He played when the mood was on him, lifting his fiddle, closing his eyes – and we were away. Once, in the little theatre at the request of the last surviving lover of Raymond Duncan, he did the lot – 'Black Eyes' and 'Coachman, Don't Speed the Horses', and any number of Cossack dances.

He wasn't better or anything. He was going to end up badly, that was for sure. But who wasn't? He still dodged Germans, he still hid out under the eaves, he still had to be fed and hosed down from time to time. But the singing dog had a career, and the house had a resident virtuoso. We left his concerts humming.

Gus

Behind a moat filled with clean green water lived a gorilla. In his enclosure was a swing made from an old tractor tyre and a hill built of fake rocks, with a little cave halfway up the rise where he could rest from the hot sun. A ramp led up the back of the hill to the rear door of the gorilla's cave. This was the keeper's entrance.

The gorilla had come many miles, from mountains and forest, to this flat veld of Johannesburg. His provenance was printed on a rusted sign on the rim of his enclosure:

RWANDAN
HIGHLAND
GORILLA

That was all. But by some means or other, this huge, dark, pensive creature got to be known to everyone as 'Gus' or, in some of the fond alternatives, he was 'good old Gus' and 'our friend Gus'.

The chimp may be our nearest simian relative but no one beats the gorilla for eliciting empathy. To stand in front of Gus, as we did, was to be impressed by his sheer attractive power. I have read that some American presidents also have this ability and I can see why this might be so – they're large, powerful and singular and their magnetic presence blots out things people prefer not to think about. When Gus turned on you his frown of concern it felt as though you were the only person in the zoo. He'd stand on his side of the moat and look you hard in the eyes, like he was aching for someone to come along and understand what he was trying to say. Something really useful, I felt sure, if only we could work out what it was.

Now and then someone swore blind he had heard Gus say something, and someone else would call out, 'I hear you, Gus,' or 'What's on your mind, big fellow?' And then more people standing outside his enclosure would hear it too and begin swaying and chanting. It was like a revivalist meeting.

Jo'burg was always a nervy place. But the silent watchers outside the gorilla enclosure pointed to something deeper. We felt a hole where our hearts should have been. It wasn't just politics or crime; it wasn't the daily tremors that tipped the teacups and the scrubbed pine dressers in Bramley and Edenvale whenever there was a rock-fall two miles down in one of the mines. It wasn't even that the Stock Exchange had moved from the city centre and had set up shop amongst the Tuscan security villages, shopping malls and sushi bars of the verdant Northern suburbs. There was electricity in the air, just as before a big thunderstorm. Our despair, which we could not identify, was mocked by the brilliant blue days and fevered buzz of this sharply chiselled city.

Those who gathered outside Gus's place came because he calmed them. He stood for something. He had something to say to them.

I was standing there one day, trying to work out what the gorilla was trying to convey, when we saw his keeper for the first time. Wearing a short white jacket and a straw hat, toting a pail, the keeper must have come into the cage by the gate into the little cave, halfway up the fake hill. He was new to Gus, judging by the way he watched him and then glanced at us, as if to say, Hey – what do we have here?

The keeper began mucking out the cage, changing the drinking water, collecting the banana skins and bits of fruit that Gus tended to strew around the place. He looked happy in his job. I hadn't seen him in thirty years maybe, not since I knelt at the altar rails to receive his blessing and felt his soft, warm hands on my head. But it couldn't have been anyone else. Same dark hair thinly smoothed over his scalp, same bright blue eyes, same Adam's apple.

I waited till he finished with the gorilla, left the enclosure and locked the iron grille behind him. Just as he was about to set off with his bucket, I called across the moat.

'Kelvin Bailey?'

And he looked hard at me and said, 'Hello, Graham,' just like that. And his look seemed to ask, Why so shocked?

And I was. It had been a long time. Decades. We had been at school together, in the parish of St Mary Magdalene in Orange Grove. Kelvin was virtually a minister from the moment he could walk. A boy priest. That's what he was good at. Kelvin didn't do sport, he didn't play kick the can or spin the bottle, or postman's knock with other people's sisters, he never kissed a girl behind the parish hall. He didn't do girls, he didn't do smoking or drinking, and when rock 'n' roll arrived, he didn't do that either. He did God and algebra.

The Baileys had lived in a little house down a long drive, and a giant loquat tree half hid the house. The family was half-hidden too. They were all quiet and good. Mrs Bailey, soft and pale, did the flowers in the church. Mr Bailey looked liked he had been carved out of wood and varnished. He was a Knight of da Gama, and took the collection in church. Kelvin's sister was Margaret, the first girl I ever fell in love with. I wrote down on a piece of paper, 'I, Graham Turner, love Margaret Bailey with all my heart, so help me God. Signed, in the year of grace, 1959.' I walked along the pavement, kicking stones, and said it over and over. One day I lost that bit of paper and worried like mad that someone was going to pick it up and read it and know all about me.

The Baileys marched in every Corpus Christi procession, when the faithful followed the shining ciborium in which was displayed the Sacred Host. And everyone who wasn't of the faith turned out of their houses to watch us pass and laughed when we knelt down on the street to pray.

To our way of thinking Kelvin was, well, *old*. He wore cycle clips to preserve his grey flannels and carried his bicycle pump into class and locked it in his desk. He was good at maths and gave me extra lessons in quadrilateral equations. He was very kind about it all. 'You're a pumpkin in matters mathematical,' he told me. I'd never been called a pumpkin before. If anyone else had said that, I'd have punched him. But coming from Kelvin, it was OK. It was so... elderly, as if he was my great-uncle or something, so it just didn't really matter.

He was a proto-priest from the time he could crawl. That was his destiny. He started as an altar boy and moved up to being Master of Ceremonies when he was eleven, a phenomenal ecclesiastical ascent. Kelvin served the priest and the priest served God. Kelvin was one of us but he was on the other side of the altar rails on holy ground. He knew the business. He joined his hands together perfectly, he bowed, he genuflected, he carried things, he rang the bells, while we sat in the pews or stood or knelt when we were told to. He was serene and shining and close to God, he was knowledgeable about how to handle incense in the thurible and holy water in the aspergillum, and where exactly to place the golden pattern on the altar. He stood beside the priest who was saying Mass and really you couldn't tell the difference. Except Kelvin was shorter, of course. The light from the stained-glass window of St Michael and the Dragon would be thrown in Technicolor on to the snowy screen of his surplice – like the fingerprint of God. And it surprised no one when he became a priest, except perhaps to leave us with the feeling that that he'd been that all along.

We had lost touch. I was living somewhere else but one day I went home and by chance I heard he was to be ordained and I turned up to witness something that had for so long been a foregone conclusion. When the ceremony was over I went up to the altar rails for his blessing, never thinking that he would remember. I knelt there, as I'd done years and years before when we had been servers together, and as he got to me he paused ever so slightly and then very gently he laid his hands on my head and spoke the blessing. He'd recognized me after all that time – it was uncanny.

And now I recognized him, and it was more than uncanny, it was unreal. But there he was – smiling the old, holy Kelvin smile.

But now I was bewildered. I could not put the keeper in the straw hat together with my friend in the dog collar. The gap seemed much too wide.

'It is Kelvin, isn't it?'

'It is Graham, it is.'

The gorilla was watching us, frowning hard.

'You working here, Kelvin?'

'I am, Graham.' He held up the bucket as if this were proof of something entirely unremarkable. Which of course it was not.

'You left the church?'

'Not the church, the priesthood.'

'What happened? Did you marry or something?'

'Didn't do either. I just stopped wanting to be a priest. So I left. I went to the jungles of Rwanda and I studied the mountain gorilla.'

'You stopped being a priest and went into gorillas?'

'It isn't so strange.' He looked at me in that sweet fashion of his. 'Not when you really think about it. After all, what does the priest, or the pastor, really do? What is the essence of pastoral faith and the Christian message?'

I had no idea what the essence of pastoral faith was but I did feel foolish standing there debating it, while a man with a bucket who used to be a priest talked to me as if it was the most natural thing in the world. All the while the gorilla kept on watching us, like *he* knew the essence of pastoral faith and longed to tell me. He wore an encouraging, you-can-do-it sort of look.

'What did Christ say?' Kelvin asked in the same gentle tone with

which he'd once asked me the value of 'x' in a quadrilateral equa-
tion.

It was another test I was going to fail.

The gorilla sat down on the tractor tyre hanging from a rope,
and turned head over heels a few times but he kept his eyes on us.

'You got me there, Kelvin. What did Christ say?'

Kelvin smiled again. 'Feed my lambs; feed my sheep. Right? So
being pastoral means protecting, looking after, keeping safe. And if
sheep need shepherding, then what about great apes? Up in
Rwanda there has been war and poaching and population explosion and habitat loss. The gorillas are suffering. So, Christ says to
us, "Feed my apes." Protect them. Or we're in great danger of losing
them for ever. It's not so strange.'

Not so strange… Here was Kelvin explaining to me why he'd
started off in a dog collar and ended up in a gorilla's cage. But, yes,
in this town, it was not so strange. Mad maybe, but not strange.

One Saturday morning some weeks later I was standing amongst
the congregation gathered outside Gus's enclosure. We were
watching and waiting, as we always were, for what exactly we did
not know. Kelvin had just finished cleaning out the enclosure. Gus
had gone inside his little cave after taking a long slow swing on his
tractor tyre and I remember someone calling out as he went inside,
'You having fun, Gus?'

Suddenly, a guy came running very fast along the tarred
pathway. He didn't stop at the seals, or the chimps, he didn't look
at the okapi – he ran on towards us, and he was carrying a gun.

Next came the cops, who were also waving guns. You could see
on the faces of the people watching Gus that they were pretty put

126

out. I mean, when you went to the zoo on a Saturday morning you did not expect the usual mayhem. There was enough robbery and violence and hijacking in the week. You went to the zoo for peace and quiet.

The gunman must have run round the back of Gus's place and found the keeper's door because next thing we saw he was right inside Gus's enclosure and he'd grabbed hold of Kelvin, pressing the gun to his head and yelling, 'If anyone comes near me, this guy gets it!'

We were all on the other side of the trench and we were thinking, Hey, why would anyone go near him? He's in big trouble as it is. Doesn't he see who is looking at him?

A little kid in the crowd kept saying, 'Look, Mommy, there's a man with a gun in Gus's house.'

That's when Gus came out of his house. The guy grabbed Kelvin even tighter and waved him back, but Gus wasn't going back. He stopped and shook his head as if to say, No, no, no. Like this wasn't the sort of thing he expected to see in his front garden. Then he beat his chest, trying really hard to give the gunman every chance to see he'd made a mistake. Then he put out his hand, as if to say, Give me the gun, OK? But the gunman wasn't listening. He was probably thinking, like a typical Jo'burger, that this gorilla wasn't being reasonable. He was thinking that the damn monkey was giving him serious uphill. So he did what any citizen did when discussions broke down and he was carrying a weapon capable of tearing holes in people – he threatened to blow Gus's head off.

But Gus still wasn't listening. He shook his head and kept on coming. The guy with the gun let go of Kelvin and levelled the pistol and told Gus to freeze, his voice getting higher. Gus kept coming.

On our side of the moat people were yelling, 'Don't shoot, don't shoot!'

It must have begun to dawn on the gunman that he wasn't dealing with a normal victim. He was facing a gorilla who didn't seem to understand what his gun meant and kept on coming, like he wanted to make a citizen's arrest...

We heard the first shot, then another, and without taking his eye off the shooter Gus went down slowly on one knee, on the other knee, and then fell face first, with the guy still screaming at him to freeze in a voice so high he have could been a soprano. The little boy was saying, 'Look, Mommy, Gus fell down. He's dead.'

There was pandemonium. The cops broke into the enclosure, the gunman had nowhere to go, more cops lined up on our side of the moat, pointing their guns. Gus was on the ground, blood was pooling and the crowd was yelling, 'He killed Gus! Take him out! Shoot the bastard!'

Some people had their cellphones out and were calling everyone they could think of – the papers, the paramedics, the Medivac chopper, the flying squad, the morgue, their mothers, each other. Every so often someone would yank the phone from his ear and yell at the cops, 'Take the bastard out!'

The cops clubbed him to the ground and handcuffed him. One cop knelt on his head. Kelvin was kneeling next to Gus, trying to staunch the bleeding. Then the helicopter was overhead and put down inside the deer park. As Gus was stretchered to the chopper, with Kelvin holding the plasma bottle, people put away their cellphones and started hugging each other and weeping.

Next day the headlines on Louis Botha Avenue and Oxford Road were full of it. It seemed it began with an attempted rape in a house a few blocks away from the zoo. Nothing too unusual there. But it had gone wrong and the young victim had run screaming into the road just as a police patrol was passing. The suspect took off, waving a pistol, and headed into the zoo. The rape itself would not have rated more than a mention well back in the paper – it was what happened when the rapist got into Gus's cage that made headlines.

> *Gorilla Nabs Gunman*
> *Monkey Business in Jo'burg Zoo*
> *Gus Makes Monkey Out of Rapist*

The gorilla enclosure looked sad and empty. People came by to stand for a few minutes in silence. Some brought gifts.

The hospital issued bulletins every twelve hours: Gus was serious but stable; Gus was out of Intensive Care. More and more people came down to the zoo and they stopped at Gus's enclosure and there they piled up a wall of flowers, a metre high. Kelvin was there every day, arranging the great wall of floral tributes, wooden crosses and soft toys given by the many kids who had together fielded an entire menagerie of fluffy chimps, baboons and gorillas. There were prayers and candlelit vigils. People said, 'I know how the British must have felt when Princess Di was killed.'

Lots of people were partial to dying animals but sceptical about prayer. There was the time they prayed for puppy Milo who had to have a heart transplant and six surgeons operated and Milo didn't make it and there was universal mourning.

'Puppy Milo Breathes His Last' said the headlines.

But Gus made it, and people were proud. It showed what concerted prayer and hope could do when local citizens pulled together. All sorts of important visitors came to see Gus in hospital. Miss South Africa came and the Minister of Safety and Security, and on Oxford Road and Louis Botha Avenue the headlines sang their dark bubbling songs:

Nation Hails Hairy Hero
Beauty Greets Beast
Minister Vows Crime Crackdown

And Kelvin was like a prophet, a wandering John the Baptist. He was at the gorilla enclosure every day, talking to people, calming them, telling them that Gus loved them and thanking them for their concern. When he led the prayers, there was all the majesty I'd seen in him back in the days when he'd been MC at High Mass and swung the thurible of incense and rang the bell. Each day, he'd gather up the fruit, the cash, the toys, one of those silver scooters, a punch bag – even a television. He'd post reports of Gus's progress on the fence of the enclosure, and everyone counted the days till Gus came home.

When it happened there were unprecedented scenes at the zoo. People marched, they sang, they carried banners that said, 'Welcome Home, Gus! And God Bless you, Big Fellow.' Gus seemed happy to be back, if a little bemused by all the razzmatazz. He lifted his hand to his eyes when he was being photographed and gave a little wave or a salute, almost a blessing. Maybe he was just shielding his eyes from the camera flashes. But it excited the crowd. 'Good old Gus,' people called out; and, perhaps most moving of all, 'Gus for President.'

Each day Kelvin would give Gus a ride on his tyre swing and Gus would knit his hands together under his chin and stare into the crowd as he went up and down. After the violence of daily life, here was someone good and pure and kind, someone who had risked his life to tackle the rapist. People were proud of him: he made a difference. After taking his swing, Gus would wave and everyone would clap, the way they do when they see the Pope.

The crowds were very big now and those who kept vigil were hoping that Gus would say something. Kelvin understood this desire and he'd say, 'Gus thanks you folks, but really he doesn't need these gifts, and if he doesn't say anything I believe we can safely say he's just pleased to be home.'

I don't know how it might have ended – because when you got down to it, Gus was a gorilla and we were Jo'burgers. But how to plumb the mystery? Kelvin was helping people to come to terms with things. He explained, gently, that Gus was not going to save the nation, he wasn't going to stamp out crime, he wasn't going to run for President.

'Thing is,' said Kelvin, in one of his little homilies, 'Gus knows you love him, but you must realize that he can't do it all for us. We have to learn to help ourselves. We're looking for some sort of miracle, but Gus does not work that way. He shows us how to be, he tackles the rapist, he risks his life, and he encourages us by his example. Look at him. Is Gus angry? He is not. Is he eaten up with hatred? Far from it. Let me tell you that Gus would willingly visit

131

his assassin, the man who tried to gun him down, just like the Pope called on the man who shot him in order to forgive him. What lesson do we think there is here for us? What is Gus trying to say to us?'

We all looked at Gus, swinging up and down, eating a banana, and he looked at us and we wondered what lesson he had for us.

I didn't go really along with Kelvin's papal analogy. The Pontiff, after all, was God's representative on earth. Gus was not like the Pope. If anyone took the papal role in this complex picture, it was Kelvin. He was Gus's representative on this side of the bars – he spoke for him, interpreted his designs and preached his message. Gus was a figure over and above his creation, who allowed his creatures free will, even if they abused it, and who was prepared to suffer and die for his creation.

But I knew a small miracle when I saw one. Some say this town is a hard-boiled place, but Guy softened its granite heart. Some say this is a city whose god is gold. Or the gun, or golf, as some wit once said. Well, for a while this was a city whose god was Gus.